WHAT BECAME OF
ANNA BOLTON

by

LOUIS BROMFIELD

CASSELL

and Company Limited
London, Toronto, Melbourne
and Sydney

BOOK
PRODUCTION
WAR ECONOMY
STANDARD

THIS BOOK IS PRODUCED IN
COMPLETE CONFORMITY WITH THE
AUTHORIZED ECONOMY STANDARDS

First published in Great Britain 1945

MADE AND PRINTED IN GREAT BRITAIN BY
MORRISON AND GIBB LTD., LONDON AND EDINBURGH
F. 1244

WHAT BECAME OF
ANNA BOLTON

WHAT BECAME OF

ANNA BOLTON

IT WAS in London in June of 1937—a London none of us will ever see again, a London in which the nineteenth century and sometimes even the eighteenth was just around the corner, for in London historical time has always lagged and one era over-lapped another. Dorchester House and Grosvenor House were gone, it is true, and in their places rose skyscraper hotels, but in Berkeley Square and Hill Street, in Bruton Street and Park Lane the nineteenth and eighteenth centuries still lingered. They lingered too in the clubs, in great houses in Kensington, in shops in Jermyn Street, and in the minds and ideas of certain people from the costermonger to the Lord Privy Seal. Because they lingered, there was still in London something called " The Season," which meant roughly the months of June and July. But even " The Season " was a memory of the nineteenth century when people who had stayed all the rest of the year in the chill green dampness of great estates in Oxfordshire and Northumberland or the Midlands " came up to London " for the balls, the dinners, the Court Receptions, and to marry off gangly girls more used to tweeds and hunters than to Worth gowns and tiaras.

In the thirties England was worried and a little tired and confused, and in the distance just a little way ahead lay, like a mirage that was all too real, the prospect of another war, a war which was certain to bring down in ruins for ever all the splendour, the sober extravagance, the folly, the tradition, that was London " in season." One war had undermined and threatened it. Another would end it. I think that all London from the King and Mr. Chamberlain down to the Pearly King in Camden Town was aware of this, however much it thrust the sense of dread into the background. It was aware, too, that England was not able really to fight a war. She was not able really to threaten the rising power of a man called Adolf Hitler.

I think that with the dread of the people was mingled the knowledge that they had no longer any leader but only a troupe of tired politicians, caught in the toils of their own weary game, men already nervous and shaken by the knowledge that their efforts to arrest time itself, to keep all those things which went into the making of " The Season," had failed, and that ahead lay only disaster. That unspoken, unacknowledged dread produced a kind of hysteria which made those last Junes before the end of the world the most brilliant England had ever known. It was as if London meant to put on a tremendous show, like the tragi-comic exposition in Paris which was closed before it was fully built, to bluff all other nations with a sense of power and splendour and importance.

But there was something un-British, something un-solid about the whole spectacle, something of the garish atmosphere of a carnival. The whole thing was *too* international and too cosmopolitan. Society was divided between those who would receive Ribbentrop and those who would not, between those who welcomed the Soviet Ambassador and those who believed him to be the Ambassador of the Devil. All the bars were down in those last three or four years. Political talk, quarrels, and recriminations filled the air at every dinner. One met swindlers from the Continent, kept women, spies and propaganda agents, refugees from Austria and from Germany itself at every dinner and ball. London is essentially British, far more British than Paris is French or Rome is Italian, and about the spectacle of cosmopolitan colourful London there was something over-wrought and frantic and unreal. The noon train at Victoria came to be known in the Ritz as the Vienna Express because of the swarms of refugees, half of them shady or pitiful and penniless adventurers, who arrived by it each day.

It may have been that the improbable carnival of the Continent, which had been in progress night and day since the Armistice of 1918, was spilling over at last into England. Some people have thought that Anna Bolton's story was too melo-dramatic, too highly coloured for reality, yet it was a pale commonplace history beside so many stories that happened in Europe during the long, disorderly armistice between the wars, stories that were all badly over-dramatized, yet all of them true.

[6]

They were stories which only sober history can tell, with any hope of being believed.

The long series began with the story of Rasputin, surviving prussic acid and bullets, who had to be pushed through a hole in the ice of the frozen Neva before he would die. That story I have heard from one of the assassins—how the poison had no effect, how bullets did not kill him, how his still living body was thrown into a sleigh waiting in the courtyard of a St. Petersburg palace lighted by torches and driven off to the river. And before his death there was all the scandal surrounding him and the Tsarina and the women of the Court. After his death his assassins never slept in a room where the lights did not burn all night. Ruin and death pursued them one by one. All bad melodrama, all cheap and tawdry, all the worst kind of cinema, but all of it true.

And it is true, too, that the Tsar of all the Russias was shot to death with the Tsarina and the Tsarevitch and the Grand Duchesses in the cellar of a commonplace *bourgeois* house in Ekaterinburg where they had been prisoners for many months.

In those same years, a man called Kreuger victimized half the world, including great bankers and whole governments, and finally shot himself with a target pistol in a flat in the Avenue Matignon in Paris. And a little while afterwards an adventurer and former pimp, under the false name of Stavisky, swindled half France, compromised the French Government, very nearly caused a revolution and civil war and finally died in a chalet half-way up a mountainside in Haute Savoie. Some said he killed himself. Others said he was shot at the orders of the Corsican Chief of Police in Paris, because the men who ruled France dared not bring him to trial and let him talk.

In the same years the King of England, Emperor of India, a descendant of the Stuarts, stepped up to a microphone and announced to Europe, Asia, Africa and America that he was abdicating his throne, " for the woman I love."

And there was the King of Spain, descendant of Charles the Fifth and last of the Hapsburg rulers, living in a boarding-house in Rome and driving through the streets in an old Ford, and little Dollfuss bleeding to death on a crimson sofa in the Chancellery in Vienna. In Rumania a King and his mistress fled with a fortune in gold and jewels in a bullet-riddled train made up of *wagon-lits* borrowed from the Orient Express; and there were all the traitors in Paris, who, acting like characters in a drama by Sardou, plotted and sold their country.

And there was Rome itself which, towards the end, became again the Rome of Caligula, of the Borgias, with intrigues and assassinations and duels and thievery and incest.

And there was the improbable story of a man called Thyssen, one of the greatest of industrial kings, who fled across the German border with only the clothes on his back to disappear later, murdered perhaps, like any penniless, unknown vagrant. And in London a great newspaper king was sued by a female international spy, who bore one of the greatest of Austrian names, for services in attempting to place his son on the ancient throne of Hungary.

In France, Reynaud and Daladier, who took turns at being Prime Minister, had mistresses (called the Countess de Portes and the Marquise de Creussol). One was the daughter of a Marseilles soap manufacturer, the other the daughter of a sardine king. Both women loved power and hated each other and intrigued at the expense of European peace and security as viciously as Pompadour or Du Barry. When the game was lost, the Countess de Portes, baffled and insane, still hungry for power, stood in the pouring rain in the courtyard of the Hotel de Ville, at Bordeaux, calling out the cars of Cabinet Ministers like a policeman. A few hours later she was dead, nearly decapitated by a steel cable stretched in the darkness across a road in the Landes to destroy her and her lover, the ex-Prime Minister, who were fleeing to Spain with a trunk of gold and secret papers.

And strangest of all there was a mad, sinister, vagrant who took the name of Hitler.

That was the Europe of the period between wars, good material for sober histories, but bad for writers of novels because it was too impossible, too vulgar, too like the pages of a sensational Sunday supplement. It was not material for an adult reader until set down in the cold, precise terms of the historians. They could one day write of it as Gibbon wrote of the Decline and Fall of Rome, as Strachey, who would have loved such florid material, wrote of Philip the Second, of Elizabeth and Catherine de Medici.

It was in this world that Anna Bolton moved. To her the people of that night-and-day carnival which preceded the invasion of Poland were people exactly like the people she knew in her home town of Lewisburg so far as flesh and blood and hair was concerned. She could talk to them and see them and touch them. Their strangeness lay in what had happened to them, how the times had moulded them, corrupting their sense of value, their morals, forcing them to live as adventurers in a melodrama. It is true, too, that they helped to mould the times, adding the luridness of Bengal lights to the whole spectacle. And to Anna it *was* a spectacle. Until the whole thing began to disintegrate, it was for Anna like sitting perpetually in a theatre box watching a corrupt but breathless play.

She did not belong *in* the piece. She would have done much better in the Europe of Edward VII. She came upon the scene too late, when the scenery was already torn and bedraggled, the actors tired and the shabby curtain about to come down for ever.

In that London season, I went to dine one June evening with Geoffrey and Ruby Hillyer. It was one of those long English twilights when the weather was clear and in Piccadilly and the West End the streets were filled with hatless men in white ties, and tails, and women in evening clothes, their evening make-up garish and hard in the clear daylight. Geoffrey was in the government, and under-secretary to the minister for the Colonies, and although he had no money of his own he was, like so many Tories, married to a rich wife whose grandfather had made a fortune in the Midlands out of manufacturing everything in the way of pottery from Wedgwood to beer mugs. They lived in a very handsome house in Hill Street, and when I arrived, most of the guests were already assembled and drinking cock-tails, all save old Mostyn Jones, who represented the nineteenth century and was politically on the shelf.

Ruby Hillyer was what was known in those days as "a hostess." That was something special, and it meant hard work and as much thought as a well-managed political campaign, for if you were a hostess you had to plan every luncheon and dinner weeks in advance in order to get exactly the right mixture of cabinet ministers and actresses, scientists and refugees, notori-ous men and kept women, with just a touch of " county " and dowdy respectability. That was the recipe for a good dinner " in season " in the London of the thirties. The famous or titled refugees frequently made things extremely difficult for the professional hostess because they were always arriving suddenly without warning, closely pursued by the Gestapo, and so there was always a great struggle to snatch them up before other hostesses discovered they were in town.

It was hard work and Ruby Hillyer really worked at the job. That was why she was one of the two most famous hostesses in London. She succeeded where others failed because she had wonderful food and wines, a beautiful and comfortable house, perfectly trained servants who had been with her for years, and knew every trick of the game and the exact social value of every guest. Also she produced the goods. She did not, like so many ambitious hostesses, use names for bait which never appeared. She did not say to you, " You must dine with me on Thursday next because Winston and the Prince are coming," and then receive you into the midst of a group of commonplace and unexciting people, all disappointed because they were only meeting each other. If she promised you Winston and the Prince, Winston and the Prince were there.

I think that by her persistence she terrified even the greatest and most irresponsible of spectacular people. And she had another of the talents of a great hostess ; she very nearly obliterated herself and her own personality. She did not, like pretentious women, invite distinguished and brilliant and spectacular people merely to listen to the outpourings of her own vain and shallow mind. She listened, and if there was a lull in the conversation, she threw in some provocative remark from the head of the table which started things going. As a result you not only nourished your body on wonderful food and wine but you heard wonderful and witty conversation, which left you, as you stepped out into Hill Street, excited and stimulated.

And often enough you heard more than mere conversation. At Ruby's table ambassadors and cabinet ministers, scientists and admirals sometimes revealed things which could not have been learned elsewhere. One had first-hand descriptions of meetings with Hitler or Dollfuss or Laval or George Bonnet. At Ruby's table I gathered the first intimations of all the misery which lay ahead of Europe and the world. There were times when in listening to the talk you were overcome with the naïveté, the folly, the stupidity, the evil, the triviality of the men in whose hands rested the fate of millions of simple, honest people.

A few people, usually less successful hostesses or people not on Ruby's list, mocked her as a "lion-hunter," but the criticism was unjust and false, like all criticism born of envy. Ruby did a remarkable job. Many an international friendship began at her table, many a policy was formulated in a corner of the big Georgian drawing-room of the house in Hill Street. Even when the war finally came and the great lunches and dinners were no longer possible and Ruby's money was mostly gone, she was undefeated. Although she was no longer young, she went to work in the War Office and none worked harder, and she managed still to bring people together, no longer at the big house in Hill Street, but in a little house in Westminster. She will have her place in the history of the spectacular times in which she lived.

She was rather a small woman, commonplace in appearance. If you passed her on the street or saw her out of her own background you would have found nothing remarkable about her. She dressed neatly and in a conventional fashion and had a face that was simply a face, and hair-coloured hair which she wore in rather a fussy coiffure always the same. It was the intensity of her brown eyes and the determination of the mouth and chin which gave you the clue to her ambition and capacity for perfection. I think the secret of her success lay perhaps in the happy combination of circumstances. Behind the sophistication, the worldliness which she had herself acquired lay the sturdiness, the snobbery, the persistence, the naïveté, the insensibility of the solid middle class of England. In her world, or in any world, that was a combination not to be defeated.

They were a perfect team, Ruby and Geoffrey, for each complemented the other. Geoffrey was tall and thin and fiftyish, with very long feet and hands and a long head. The traditional ideas of his class were embedded in the brilliance of his mind like a cairngorm diamond in a setting of platinum. Second cousin of a duke, with his wife's fortune to give him not only security but affluence, he was a natural adjunct to the Tory Party and so was always taken care of by a place, not too important, in every Tory government.

The dinner that evening was typical of the time and background. In addition to the venerable Mostyn Jones, there was present a well-known lady, quites imply a tart, with certain superior qualities, who had done very well for herself. She had secured two substantial settlements from rich men and on the strength of them married an impecunious and complacent and decadent old peer. They lived in the same house but never went to the same parties. He liked music and the ballet and she liked Ciro's and the Four Hundred Club. She was small, blonde and fading, despite every desperate effort. She had the Rabelaisian wit of a good barmaid and a genuine talent for telling a shady story.

And there was Bertram Hodley, who briefly was a big man in the Board of Education, with his dowdy but faithful wife, Pansy, and Prince Altemberg, one of the more recent arrivals by the Vienna Express, a dark and handsome fellow who had helped to organize the opposition to the Socialists and then had run foul of Dollfuss and Schuschnigg and the Catholics. And there was Jean de Cyon, one-legged veteran of the last war, from the French Embassy, and Lily Ainsworth, the actress, a fine handsome woman of sixty, who had played Shakespeare with Beerbohm Tree and knew everyone and went everywhere. Each one was invited for a special reason. Each one was a part of a recipe then in fashion for a good London dinner in season. I was there as a foreign correspondent of *The Times* because a writer or a journalist with any sort of name was always a part of the recipe.

There was nothing remarkable about the dinner. Mostyn Jones who had known everybody in politics for the past sixty years might have been amusing in a vitriolic fashion, but he seemed tired and suffering from indigestion, and despite all Ruby Hillyer's attempts to draw him, he yielded only a little discreet flatulence. Lady Kernogan told a story of which the last line was, "Tut! Tut! Mind your etiquette," which fell rather flat. Old Mostyn Jones chuckled wickedly and Pansy Hodley looked bewildered. Ruby herself did not approve. From her forced smile you could see that she felt this was one of the times when Lady Kernogan had outdone herself.

It was no better after dinner. When the ladies rejoined the gentlemen in the big high-ceilinged drawing-room, Ruby said, "We're all invited to a party Anna Bolton is giving at Haddonfield House." She laughed, "I'm not trying to drive you all out of the house—but the party will be fun. Everybody will be there. She asked me to bring all of you after dinner. It won't really begin until midnight."

At once something happened to the party. Very likely it

[12]

was the name of Anna Bolton and the prospect of a human story. We had been talking all the evening in a tired way, mostly about politics and abstractions, and now suddenly a character had been projected into our midst, and mystery and gossip and the prospect of a good story.

Ruby added, " Sybil Haddonfield is giving the party with her."

" And Mrs. Bolton is paying for it," said Lady Kernogan.

It seemed that everyone in the room knew her, at least by name, save Pansy Hodley, who although she got around quite a bit in London, was really interested only in her garden and the Girl Guides in her own county and never registered any worldly gossip. Even old Mostyn Jones, up from his retreat in Wales, rather perked up and said, " They say she's a good-lookin' woman."

And then they began to talk about Anna.

It was natural that Ruby should know her and refer to her as " Anna " rather than as Mrs. Bolton, for Anna was beginning to be someone—one of those who had to be included in dinners that Ruby gave. Ruby, of course, knew a great deal about her, for as a professional hostess she had made a kind of investigation, but much of her information was wrong. It was derived largely from those apocryphal stories which had begun to circulate concerning Anna's wealth, her looks, her furs, her jewels, the mystery of her background. It was all very vague and contradictory and coloured by the quality of fantasy which surrounds the personality of spectacular people who become in time legendary. Boiled down, it came about to this—that Anna Bolton was American, that she was about thirty-four or thirty-five years old, that she was fabulously rich and had the finest emeralds and the blackest sables in Europe, that her money came variously from the automobile industry, from breakfast foods, from vast chains of hotels, from oil lands.

She had appeared briefly on the horizon of London a year or two earlier, and made some rather dowdy Tory friends. None of the " right sort " of Americans seemed to know her or anything about her. She had always with her a companion-secretary called Miss Godwin, who acted as a kind of sheep-dog. Miss Godwin, it appeared, was " genteel " and knew some of the best of the right people in London. And now suddenly Mrs. Bolton was a friend of the Marchioness of Haddonfield and knew important people and gave " wonderful *dee-vine* parties."

It was all of a piece with the kind of worldly, trivial gossip which one heard so much in London those last days before the end of the world.

I offered nothing. I only sat listening, behaving as a somewhat tired newspaper correspondent who knew nothing whatever about Anna Bolton. I might have had a great success. I might have become a mild sensation and the centre of attraction, but I was, for once at least, chivalrous and held my tongue. The truth was that in the whole room I was the only one who really *knew* anything about Anna Bolton. What I kept seeing was not the rich woman with the most famous emeralds in Europe, but a handsome girl of sixteen in a white shirt blouse and a rather threadbare skirt who came up from the Flats of Lewisburg, Ohio, to occupy the seat opposite me in Latin class at the high school. I kept saying to myself, " Keep your mouth shut. Let her get away with it. Let her have her fun. It's what she wanted . . . always. Keep your mouth shut and let Annie Scanlon have her fun."

And so I sat silently, a little amused, a little curious, listening to speculations and stories about Anna having been a Follies girl or a governess or a model. They were all stories very far off the beam, but it was clear that Anna must *really* be someone to arouse so much interest, so much speculation.

And then the door opened and the head housemaid (for Ruby never had men servants), a tall grenadier of a woman, opened the drawing-room door and announced, " Major Von Kleist ! "

The man who came in was tall and handsome in a hard way, with the peculiar erect stiff carriage of Prussian military men. He had the peculiarly " clean " appearance that one finds frequently in people of bad conscience who are always physically bathing or being manicured as if to wash away the sins of the spirit. He had a rather large head with dark hair, greying a little on the temples. The eyes were small and grey, the nose straight and narrow, the chin large and firm and the mouth too thin and straight to be sympathetic. There was an air of distinction about him, that peculiarly obvious German distinction which is touched by brutality and a lack of all intuition or sensibility. You knew at once that he was German and probably Prussian. If you knew Germany well you would have said that he came very likely from Pomerania. The white tie and tails did not suit him as they suit an Englishman. He should have come through the door in the armour of the Teutonic Knights.

Most of the people in the room knew him, for he went about a good deal as one of the more civilized and presentable products of the Embassy. I was one of those acquainted with him, twice I had gone to him to secure what special information I could on military subjects. He impressed me as an intelligent man, although a little cynical and tired. The weariness was not physical, for like many German officers he kept himself in superb physical condition ; it was rather a weariness of the mind and point of view. It betrayed itself in the quiet, rather charming smile which seemed to say, " What is all the hubbub about ? What fools the human race are ! In any case there is no hope."

He was not a likeable man, for there seemed to be little warmth in him, yet there was a quality of geniality about him. If he liked you, he seemed to accept you at once without preliminary exploration or reserve. He did it deftly, a little by the way he looked at you, a little by the quality of his voice, a great deal by the way he put you at your ease. He was a great asset to the Germans at that moment because there were so few like him. Most of them were slippery and common like Von Ribbentrop or merely pompous and offensive.

Now he came into the room with great dignity and ease, lips parted with a slightly twisted smile which seemed to embrace everyone and at the same time to mock all of us in a gentle friendly way—Ruby and the Hodleys and the fading Lady Kernogan and even ageless old Mostyn Jones.

The grenadier maid brought him coffee and brandy and he explained that he was sorry about not being able to come for dinner. He had been held at the Embassy by special messages from Berlin directed to himself which had had to be decoded.

" Nothing ferocious, I hope," said Maudie Kernogan.

" Nothing ferocious," he smiled. But even his smile did not carry off Maudie's unfortunate mocking remark. It was clearly already a little late in historical times for that kind of remark to be altogether tactful, and Von Kleist was himself too intelligent a man not to have known that time was growing

[15]

short and that even in this room, where people with worldly views came together, there were those who hated him simply for being a German. I had a sense too that he was always a little ashamed of Adolf Hitler as a kind of over-played and vulgar monstrosity for whom excuses had to be made among civilized people. But he was not the type to make excuses.

Ruby whisked the conversation quickly away from Maudie Kernogan's tactless remark, saying, " We were just talking about Anna Bolton. I hope you are going with us to the ball."

" Yes," he answered, and rather stiffly added, " she is a charming woman. I've known her for quite a long time."

" Tell us about her," said Maudie with venomous eagerness.

" There's nothing to tell. I met her in Paris. I've seen quite a lot of her since then."

" I've heard so many strange stories about her," said Maudie.

" There's nothing very strange about her." It seemed to me that a little colour came into the pale face. " She's American and rich and handsome and very generous."

I don't remember the rest of the conversation because I kept seeing Annie again back in high school, in the shabby but very clean shirt blouse and skirt, and thinking how unlikely it was that I should be sitting here listening to an officer in the German army defending and even praising her.

Then suddenly Ruby rose and said, " I think we'd all better go along inasmuch as all of us are going." Then she turned to me. " Will you come with me in my car ? "

I was a little surprised, for usually under such circumstances Ruby would have taken more important persons than myself. She should have taken Mostyn Jones, an ex-Prime Minister, or Von Kleist from the German Embassy, or almost any of the others. Knowing Ruby, I suspected that she wanted something.

In the car on the way to Haddonfield House she made no effort to disguise what it was she wanted. She said abruptly, " Why were you so silent while we were talking about Anna Bolton ? I'm sure you must know all about her. You're an American who has been around."

The voice inside me again said, " Let Annie Scanlon have her fun ! " and I lied quietly, " I really know nothing about her. I met her once long ago in New York. Her husband was still alive. He was a nice old gentleman of about sixty, or sixty-five, an inventor who happened also to be a good business man. That's all I know."

"Why didn't you say even that much?"

I grinned, "Because it seemed so much less interesting than all the stories people make up about her."

"I must say that she's been very clever about this party," said Ruby. "She didn't send out a lot of invitations to people she didn't know. She just had her secretary call up people she did know and say that she was giving a party and would you bring your guests if you were having a dinner or if you were dining out ask the other guests to come along. She knows enough key people in London and there's enough curiosity about her to bring everybody in London."

I knew how it would work. All the fashionable world of London and a considerable number of hangers-on would get the news that Anna Bolton was giving a party. They would all say, "My dear, I hear that extraordinary Mrs. Bolton is throwing a brawl Thursday night. Are you going? Of course you must. It will be *dee-vine*. They say there'll be acrobats and elephants. They say she's terrific. I scarcely know her myself but she seems all right."

That was the way it all worked. In the end Anna would have everyone. She had indeed been very clever about it.

And in the background there was another element of great importance—Anna's reported "friendship" with Lady Haddonfield. It had got round that Lady Haddonfield was Anna's great friend and sponsor. I do not know how great a friend Lady Haddonfield was, nor do I think Anna ever knew or even knows to-day. Possibly only Lady Haddonfield knows, and being Lady Haddonfield she is very likely unable to judge, since friendship as it is known to ordinary people never meant much to her in her long and ambitious career.

Out of all I knew of London I thought I understood the basis of the alliance, and I'm sure now that I was right. I could never get Anna to admit it afterwards. I think because she was ashamed of it. She would only say, years afterwards, "Lady Haddonfield was my first friend in London. She still is my friend." But I don't believe it. I believe it was a bargain made between them tacitly but with perfect and cold-blooded calculation and understanding. Anna wanted to meet everybody, to

[17]

be everything, to swallow the whole world. Lady Haddonfield could help her.

What Lady Haddonfield wanted was simple and straight-forward enough. It was the greatest need of women of her class in those days, and perhaps all through English history. She simply wanted money. In the period of the long armistice between the wars the well-born Englishwoman's desire for money was sharpened by terrific death-duties and devastating taxes. A good many of them in the so-called upper classes became as voracious as girls in a Port Said brothel.

It was not that Lady Haddonfield was poor. She was not one of those destitute "Gentlewomen in distress" who advertised in *The Times* that for a consideration she would introduce strangers to titled people. On the contrary, the Marchioness of Haddonfield was wealthy and politically one of the most powerful women in England. She was, one might have said, a woman who had very nearly everything. She was born the daughter of a peer and cabinet minister. At nineteen she had married the Marquess of Haddonfield, a rich man with one of the great English titles. At fifty she was a handsome woman who loved politics and intrigue and was considered the greatest hostess of the Tory Party, so great a hostess that she had been credited with corrupting at least two leaders of the Labour Party and of leading them into collaboration with the Tories.

But she was also a woman of boundless ambition and she intended, if it were humanly possible, that her husband should one day be Prime Minister. The only fly in the ointment was that Lord Haddonfield did not share her ambitions and was not a very intelligent politician.

As the Marchioness of Haddonfield and a political woman she had great obligations, not the least of which was the maintenance of Haddonfield House, one of the last of the great London houses to hold out against the levelling process. There were also great estates in Perthshire and in Gloucestershire which taxes had long ago turned from assets to liabilities. And there were charities that were an ancient tradition of the Haddonfield family, such charities as virtually the total support of the St. Agnes Lying-in Hospital. To abandon these would have been a very bad political move. So, although the bookkeeping of the Haddonfields involved vast sums of money, the outgo was as vast as the income, and there were times when a hundred pounds

actually made a great difference one way or another. The great
Lady Haddonfield did not actually advertise in *The Times* as a
gentlewoman in distress who could introduce strangers in
England to persons of title for a consideration, but that was
exactly what she was doing in the case of Anna. The only
difference was that instead of the " consideration " being a few
pounds, it was somewhere between twenty and thirty thousand
pounds ; and the whole thing was handled far more subtly
than a cash transaction. Anna Bolton simply gave that sum to
Lady Haddonfield's charities, thus relieving the lady of that
obligation, and increasing Lady Haddonfield's income by the
same amount.

It was a neat arrangement and both women got what they
wanted by it. Twenty to thirty thousand pounds to charity was
a sum Anna could well afford since she had an immense fortune,
lived in rented houses or in hotels, and had no expenses save the
money she spent on herself. Money did not mean much to her
because there was so much of it. Knowing everyone, devouring
the whole world was far more important.

I have gone at some length into the story of Lady Haddonfield
because it explains why in that world between the two wars
almost anything was possible and why strange and improbable
combinations of people came into being. It was all part of the
story of a world in its death agonies, when all barriers were down,
and trickery and barter and desperate measures were the only
rules. It was a world that kept pulling itself up by its own bootstraps, driven always by the sense of its own doom.

Haddonfield House was one of the last magnificent remnants
of Georgian London. The Haddonfields could no longer afford
to keep it open the year round and had long since made it a
practice to lease it to rich foreigners during " The Season."

It was warm that evening and the great doors stood open,
revealing the broad stairway which led up to the drawing-room
and ballroom. I thought, " How much longer will it last ? "
I know now that we will never again in our times see the sort of
spectacle we saw that night—flunkeys in powdered wigs and
white hose, all the men in white ties and tails, the women
wearing Paris gowns and covered with jewels.

As I walked up the stairs I thought, " And Annie from the
wrong side of the tracks will be standing there at the top of the

stairway." And then another thought occurred to me. "Will she remember me? Will she pretend not to know me as an old schoolmate?"

She did not know I was coming. She had not invited me. She probably did not even know I was in London. I was being brought by the Hillyers. Did she even know that I had become mildly famous as a correspondent of *The Times*? I had not seen her for ten years and then only for a moment in the lobby of the Ritz in New York.

We came to the top of the stairs. I stepped behind Ruby Hillyer who after she exchanged greetings with Lady Haddonfield said, " Do you know Mr. Sorrell?" And Lady Haddonfield said, " No. How do you do." Then the politician in her came out and she said, " You're not the famous David Sorrell, are you?" And I answered, " I don't know how famous I am, but David Sorrell is my name. I came with the Hillyers. I was dining there."

I realized that the line was being held up. Ruby was talking to Anna and I was aware of Anna standing there triumphant and handsome and hard. I was aware too that she had heard the name of David Sorrell, that she remembered it and took a quick glance to make certain. I know now that while she was making small talk with Ruby she was deciding what course to take, to remember me or pretend that she had never heard of me before. The course she took would tell me whether or not she had deliberately traded the talents she had for this bejewelled mess of pottage that surrounded her.

Lady Haddonfield went right on talking to me. " We must have a chat later on. There is so much you must know about what is going on on the Continent."

I was a newspaper man of some authority who might one day be useful in forwarding her ambitions for her husband. Also I might be able to tell her inside things about what was going on in Russia and Germany that might be of great use to her. She was not a woman to overlook things.

But the presence of the waiting people in the line behind me became very obvious, and turning to Anna, she said, " This is Mr. Sorrell . . . you know, the correspondent."

I knew those blue eyes of Annie's—that they could be warm and kindly or as cold as ice. I had seen them change in a second when that awful pride of hers was hurt. Now as they met mine they were perfectly blank of all expression. In them there was not the faintest sign of recognition or embarrassment. They betrayed nothing whatever. "That," I thought, "she has learned."

She said, "I am very glad you could come. It was good of Mrs. Hillyer to bring you."

"It was kind of you to let her bring me. Thank you," I said.

Then she turned to the woman behind me and I went on into the ballroom, thinking without bitterness, "If that's the game you want to play, it's okay with me. I won't betray you." But I couldn't help thinking, "There, side by side, receiving half of Europe, stand the two hardest, most ambitious she-devils in the world!"

Rather than any sensation of resentment, I experienced one of admiration at her performance. She had come a long way. She had become, in a sense, a new person. She was no longer wild, bad, proud Annie Scanlon. Annie Scanlon was dead. The woman receiving a gaudy, dying world at the top of the great stairway in Haddonfield House had never known Annie Scanlon. I was certain that she knew all the time that I was Dave Sorrell from Lewisburg. In the ten years since she had seen me I could not have changed beyond recognition. A man does not change much between twenty-five and thirty-five. I had changed much less than Anna herself. She had lost altogether the look of voluptuousness she had had as a girl. She still had her peculiarly racy good looks but they were fined down and hardened. She was like a fine race-horse in training.

As I turned away I saw, standing a little way behind her, an older woman of perhaps sixty. I should not perhaps have noticed her but for her remarkable air of distinction. She had a fine, narrow head with high cheek-bones and a high-bridged nose. She wore her hair drawn straight back in an uncompromising knot at the nape of her neck and wore one of those dowdy nondescript frocks of black lace which can be worn anywhere at any time and mean nothing whatever. Clearly she made not the least concession to fashion or make-up, relying solely on her look of race and character to carry her through. Yet in a way she had beauty and was the most distinguished-looking woman in the room, far more so than Anna, who had never succeeded in losing a slight look of commonness, or

Lady Haddonfield whom the years had turned into a rather handsome bony mare.

When I asked Ruby who the woman was, she said, "It is Miss Godwin, Anna's secretary. My older sister used to know her years ago as a girl. She's American and when she was young she was one of the famous beauties who came over for the season."

Then she turned and, raising her voice a little, said, "Good evening, Miss Godwin. I would like to introduce David Sorrell, a friend of mine."

Miss Godwin turned towards me with a charming but rather sad smile. She was handsomer than I had noticed at first.

We talked for a little time about nothing in particular. She asked how long I had been in London this time and where I had come from. Ruby said that the evening had all the signs of being a brilliant success and Miss Godwin's face softened a little. "Yes," she said, "it's almost like the old days when the King was still alive."

That remark fixed her at once. She was Edwardian. For Edwardians, the only King had been Edward VII. Since his day everything had been dull and slightly shabby. Then she said to Ruby, "How is your sister? It's such a long time since I've seen her."

"She's at Malcolm's Reach," said Ruby. "She doesn't come up for the season any more."

"Tell her," said Miss Godwin, "to look me up if she does come to town."

Then the major-domo came up and asked Miss Godwin if he might speak to her and we moved away. She made a great impression on me. Afterwards, I was glad that I met her that night, for she played a great rôle in Anna's life. Even now, long after she is dead, I see her face very clearly. It was not a face you forget.

The party was a great success. There was plenty of the best champagne and the two best dance bands to be found in London and a whole music-hall programme with an American torch singer, a remarkable troupe of Rumanian acrobats, Cerenova from the Monte Carlo Ballet then playing at Covent Garden, and a fantastic trained dog. The performance took place at one end of the beautiful classic ballroom and people came and went, talking rudely through much of the programme. It was a little like the entertainment by dancers which accompanies the state dinners of Maharajas in India : the dancers go on frantically dancing and gyrating while none of the guests interrupts his conversation to give them even the compliment of a glance. Most of the people there were more interested and entertained by the spectacle of themselves than by the efforts of the performers. I have long suspected that the decline of the music hall in that era, like the decline of high-class prostitution, was caused by too much amateur competition. Certainly it was difficult that evening to tell a trollop from a lady, and difficult for the music-hall artistes to compete with the general spectacle.

I had my talk with Lady Haddonfield, who " pumped " me brazenly for all information she could get concerning Moscow and Berlin. When I told her that in my opinion the policy of the Tory government was rapidly leading England towards certain ruin, she only snorted indignantly and gave the old Tory answer that a foreigner, even an American, could not possibly understand the intricacies of British politics. I smiled and said that in my opinion they did not appear intricate but merely transparent and sometimes stupid.

England was like that then—a nation with a complacent, occasionally corrupt upper class, a wretched working class and a stupid middle class, rushing merrily downhill under the leadership of a government largely made up of knaves and fools. The whole picture was only a part of the larger European spectacle.

But to Anna as to myself it was fascinating. A great deal of it Anna did not understand at all because she had neither the background nor the experience to understand it. To her it was largely a fine show, super-theatrical, in which she was playing a small rôle but one constantly growing in importance. That night she was becoming known for the first time as one of the cast.

I watched her from a distance, moving among her guests, handsome and excited. There was at times a sudden return of that childlike directness which had made her so attractive as a girl. Now and then the distinguished, rather grim, Miss Godwin approached her and spoke a word or two concerning details of the party. I was aware of two things—that consciously Anna was avoiding me, and that she was almost hysterically happy. I had, too, a suspicion, perhaps born of

[23]

my old affection for her, that she was a little ashamed of herself for pretending she didn't know me. I thought, " If only she is a little ashamed there is hope for her."

A little after two I went home, and as I walked through the big drawing-room I had a final glimpse of her talking to a cabinet minister and Lady Kernogan. She was laughing and looked extremely handsome.

Then, from out of the crowd I saw the tall straight figure and gently sardonic face of Major Von Kleist coming towards her. He stopped for a moment in the doorway, watching Anna. Believing himself unnoticed there he dropped his restraint and for a moment the small grey eyes were lighted with the kind of admiration a connoisseur has for a beautiful work of art, something which is very nearly perfect. It was not a look either of love or of passion, but one of pure admiration. It was almost as if he turned his head from side to side to examine her from all angles—the handsome figure, the slightly " touched-up " Irish red hair, the white skin, the Chanel dress of black with silver stars, the emeralds and diamonds. She represented something as a work of art which few if any American men would have understood or wholly valued. Von Kleist would know the value of the emeralds and that they were set by Cartier ; he would know that the dress came from Chanel, the slippers from Perugia. That was his business as a man of the world and a diplomat of those times, but such things also interested him passionately as a part of the brilliantly artificial whole that was Mrs. Bolton, the chic, expensive and rich Mrs. Bolton. For him there was perhaps nothing between a whore and a woman like this. That was something difficult for an American to understand—a kind of cold adoration without warmth, almost without desire. It was a part of Von Kleist's background and of his decadence, the result of a refinement, even a kind of civilization pushed too far, over the border into perversion. The fascinating thing was that in the admiring face there was always a shadow of cold brutality.

After a moment he moved out of the doorway towards Anna and as she turned towards him, he spoke to her and she gave her brilliant smile and went with him into the ballroom to dance. The Viennese band was playing the " Emperor Waltz " and for a moment I stood watching them. There were only three or four other couples on the floor beneath the Venetian glass chandeliers, so that they had the floor almost to themselves. Von Kleist waltzed like a good German and Anna as a partner was quite as good. She had always been, like most people of great vitality, a beautiful dancer. To-night she was dancing as she had never danced before, here in Haddonfield House with all the great world gathered about her.

As I watched her a vivid memory returned to me suddenly. It was the picture of Anna long ago, saying bitterly, " I'll show Lewisburg ! You wait and see, some day I'll show Lewisburg ! " And I thought, " That is really what she is doing now—she's ' showing Lewisburg.' " And Lewisburg had long since forgotten her. Probably no one from Lewisburg save myself even knew that the famous Mrs. Bolton had once been the daughter of Mary Scanlon, the charwoman.

I did not embarrass her by waiting to say good night. I went down the great stairway between the powdered footmen and out into the soft air of a fine summer night of London in June. It was so fine a night that I chose to walk all the way to the hotel. And as I walked I thought, " That is the motive of many a success in this world. Demosthenes became a great orator because he was determined to show his fellow-students that despite a defect of speech he could surpass them. Napoleon conquered Europe and changed the history of the human race because he had to ' show ' his fellow-officers that he was not an insignificant little fellow who had no success with women. Alexander Hamilton. . . ." It was the springboard of so many careers. The list was long. There was no end to it all the way from Solomon to Adolf Hitler.

In the darkness I found myself blushing because I understood suddenly that I too had gone away from home meaning to " show Lewisburg," because I wasn't good at sports in High School and was called a sissy and a weakling. In a way I wasn't any better than Anna. " Showing Lewisburg " had been my springboard. And in the darkness I felt a quick, warm understanding for the hard, bright woman standing at the head of the great stairway of Haddonfield House. I did not mind her denial of me. I didn't mind at all because I kept seeing her as a hurt, proud young girl with whom I had once been in love, with that first love which is always something special and a little ridiculous and never quite forgotten.

Lewisburg was an old town. About fifty thousand people lived there among the hills that overlooked the Ohio River. It had never been a boom town. It just grew slowly from the first settlement made by people partly from New England and partly from Virginia. It was a rich town, too, with that solid wealth which often marks American towns of that size and background. It lived largely off the rich agricultural country of which it was the capital, and from a dozen small industries, and the two trunk railroads which met there at the great bridge to cross the river. As a town it hung on to its money and stored it away. I think the principal fear of the rich families of Lewisburg was that someone, anyone, might find out how rich they really were. Towards the beginning of the century they built along Centre Avenue great houses bedecked with fretwork and towers and cupolas, and then lived in them with one servant or possibly none at all. To say that Lewisburg was a conservative town was an understatement.

It was a rich town but it had grim poverty in the Flats along the river, where each spring the water flooded the first floors of all the houses, and it had a lot of people who got along all right in a modest way, and it had two or three families like the Harrigans who made a lot of money and spent it all and didn't fit in anywhere ; but it was the families in the big houses along Centre Avenue who really ran the place, because they really owned it, banks and business buildings and factories, and about everything else that was loose.

That tiny world of comfortable, rather dull and dowdy people along Centre Avenue was a tight world and as caste-ridden as an Indian State. At the very top stood those families descended from the original settlers, who had hung on to land until it turned into big money ; a little way beneath were the families founded by newcomers who had made big money ; and just beneath them were the descendants of the original families who had lost their money and rather gone to seed. These three subdivisions belonged to one caste and their members mixed socially and intermarried.

Then there were the families who just managed to get along comfortably. The members of this group intermarried and sometimes introduced new blood by marriage with travelling salesmen or clerks who worked in the factories.

And down at the very bottom were the people of the Flats

who hadn't any caste at all and sometimes were not too strong on marriage. It just didn't enter into their scheme of things. A good many of them simply mated and had families and as often as not there wasn't anything very permanent about the mating.

Annie belonged to the people of the Flats, although she was born legitimately. However disreputable her father may have been, her mother was a fine honest woman and a good Roman Catholic.

I belonged to the third subdivision of the highest caste—the old families who had lost their money and rather gone to seed— and Tom Harrigan didn't belong anywhere at all. His father and mother were newcomers, and although his father made a great deal of money as a building contractor, the family spent it all. And, too, they were Irish Roman Catholics, which in that old Protestant town made a great difference. It didn't matter how much money they made, they still remained "outsiders." You might like people like the Harrigans but you didn't invite them to your house or marry any of them.

Anyone who has ever lived in a town like Lewisburg knows all these things. Twenty-five years ago it was much worse than it is to-day, when stress and trouble have broken down old nineteenth-century barriers.

The High School was really the only place where all the elements ever met. There were schools in various sections of the town, but the position of those who attended each school was determined by its locality. The children from the big houses on Centre Avenue went to the Centre Avenue Grade School and the middle-class children to Fleming Street and the ragged children from the Flats to Tenth Street. Annie went to grade school with the Flats children and Tom Harrigan went to Fleming Street and I grew up with the children on Centre Avenue. So the three of us never got together until we reached High School, all about the same time.

On the very first day I noticed Annie, for even then you couldn't help noticing her. She was one of only four kids that came up from the Flats. Most of those from the Flats went only as far as the eighth grade and then left school to go to work. The four from the Flats rather huddled together that first day— three rather tough overgrown boys and Annie. Afterwards the huddle broke up because two of the boys were good football players and the other played basketball, but there wasn't anything like that for Annie. In those days girls didn't go into athletics and clubs, and there wasn't any place at all for Annie Scanlon. She just remained alone.

I think the thing that was hardest for her was that everyone, herself more than any of the others, knew that she was the daughter of old one-legged Pete Scanlon who operated the crossing gates at Tenth Street until he was discharged for drunkenness, and of Mary Scanlon, the best charwoman in town. It was Mary Scanlon who was called in twice a year by the women who lived in the big ugly houses along Centre Avenue to clean, air and scrub everything in their houses. Everyone wanted Mary Scanlon. All the old families always had her. There was indeed a kind of snobbery about employing Mary. It was one of the signs of your importance.

You couldn't help noticing Annie because of her bold looks and colouring—her red hair and blue eyes and a figure developed beyond her years. It was a figure like that of a young Venus Genetrix, made for love, made for bearing children. Even the High School boys who didn't understand such things felt them by instinct. Some of the boys from Centre Avenue as they grew older would have liked to take advantage of her but, coming from the Flats, Annie had a precocious knowledge of what they were after and why they paid her attentions, and she would have none of it. They never got anywhere with her at all.

During the three years Annie went to High School she was always at the head of every class. It wasn't only that she had brains but that she used them. She was driven always by her pride and the knowledge that Mary Scanlon was determined that her daughter was to have a better life than her own had been. Again and again I saw Annie's face flush with satisfaction at being able to answer some question of algebra or geometry which none of the others in the class could answer. It wasn't that she was the teacher's pet either. Most of these teachers had their own petty snobbery, and Annie, with her flamboyant figure and colouring and her way of distracting the attention of the older boys by her mere presence, wasn't exactly the type to arouse friendliness and admiration in the breast of a spinster school teacher. Physically she was typical of the small-town " bad girl," but in the whole school there was no girl better behaved or more above reproach. I think she was meant by Nature to be the " bad girl " but her pride and resentment prevented it. The result was a kind of frustration and choked bitterness.

She refused the fumbling, adolescent advances of the High School boys from Centre Avenue and in her pride and ambition she could not take up with any of the loutish, tough boys from the Flats. Her relations with the girls were even worse. Once or twice Mary Downing, one of the girls who was kinder than the others, asked Annie to a party on Centre Avenue, but she always refused. How was it quite possible to go to a party in the house where your mother was the charwoman? She never went to school dances. By the third year in High School she was solitary, proud and bitter.

Somehow I got on better with Annie than anyone in the whole school. I think there were a good many reasons for this. One was that I didn't really belong to the Centre Avenue people among whom her mother worked. My family had a right to live there so far as the silly thing called " family " was concerned, but neither my father nor grandfather had been very smart about money and by the time I was born, my family was living off Centre Avenue, not on the wrong side of the tracks but in a vague borderland where houses were small and old and rents cheap. That blurred my social outline.

And I was sickly from the effects of scarlet fever, which left me with a bad heart so that I wasn't any good at sports. And I was shy and envied other boys who could do all the things I was never able to do, and that brought about a passion to excel in other things to justify myself. That perhaps was what really brought Annie and me together. We were the two smartest people in the High School and there was a curious friendly rivalry between us as to who could get the best marks or answer the most difficult question first. By the third year both of us could read Latin very nearly as easily as we read English. Many a time I would happen to glance towards her across the classroom and catch her blue eyes on me and she would smile, as if she were trying to say to me, " These others are all stupid fools and idiots. You and I know all these things."

The smiles encouraged me and one day after school I raised the courage to say to her, " I haven't got anything to do. Can I walk home with you?"

She looked at me with surprise and then grinned, " Why should you want to walk home with me? It's a long way down to the Flats."

I flushed and said, " I'd just like to. That's all."

"Well," she said, "there's no law against it. If you're foolish enough to want to go all the way down there."

"I do," I said.

It was a compulsion curious and puzzling to me at the age of sixteen. It was the first time that I had ever experienced any awareness of a feeling for girls. Until then boys and girls were friends and that was all, but slowly the sight of Annie and that slow understanding smile of hers had done something to the inside of me. I had to be near her. I wanted to talk to her, to translate into words the thing I found in her eyes when we smiled at each other. And I must confess that I was aware of her figure, and her colouring, and blue eyes. And I think, too, that even then, because I was myself a weakling, I had a feeling for the underdog. Rightly or wrongly I felt sorry for Annie. I wanted, with quixotic fervour, to espouse her cause. I wanted to show the others that to me it did not matter that Annie's mother was the charwoman and her father the crossing-keeper, that it did not matter that Annie lived in a shabby house in the Flats.

That night in London, as I walked across the Green Park from Haddonfield House back to my hotel, I blushed in the darkness at the memory of how, long ago, I had sometimes wakened in the night and felt warm with satisfaction over my chivalry, that I defied all the conventions of the town by being seen walking with Annie Scanlon back to her house in the Flats.

Indeed, my feelings towards Annie were very confused and vague, compounded of the first stirrings of sexual feeling, a distorted sense of chivalry, and an honest indignation at the cruelty of a world which made Annie Scanlon, with her looks and intelligence, an outsider. The trouble was that it didn't seem to be the fault of any one person. It was the fault of Lewisburg itself with all its intricate, senseless pettiness and worn-out traditions, of prejudice. It was even the fault of Annie herself. She was so stiff-necked and sensitive. She wouldn't even give me the small satisfaction of being friendly and simple. It was as if she were thinking, angrily, "You're just being kind. That's all it means !"

It was only when we talked about history that Annie seemed to turn human and simple and friendly. We both liked history and we were both very good at it, I think because neither of us found Lewisburg a very attractive or exciting place. Both of us escaped out of our unhappiness into history the way some people escape into novels, not only in our dreams but in our own conversation. Both of us liked French history best of all, I think because we both divined that in everything concerned with France there was an elegance and glamour that other history did not have. Annie liked especially the period of Francis I and the Renaissance, and I was inclined to like the eighteenth century. We argued about it a good deal, sometimes on the walks home and sometimes when I stopped in at the shabby house not far from the river front where the Scanlons lived. I think Annie identified herself with Diane de Poitiers and perhaps she was right. Certainly Diane at the height of her career must have produced much the same effect as Anna Bolton on that night at Haddonfield House—the effect which Von Kleist so openly admired.

The Scanlons' house was shabby and unpainted on the outside, with a few sooty lilacs and irises growing in the narrow door-yard. It was only a little way from the river and the railway crossing where Pete Scanlon had once operated the crossing gates. The trains seemed to go right through the house, and on winter evenings the mournful whistles of the river boats came up through the fog.

Inside, the small house was very neat and bright. How Mary Scanlon kept it so in that part of the town, I don't know. The furniture was mostly golden oak, of which Mary Scanlon was very proud, and there were a good many religious pictures. She was a small woman, full of Irish pride and superstition and good humour, with hands that were always red and cracked from lye water. Annie was an only child, born when Mary Scanlon was past thirty, and Mary always seemed more like her grandmother than her mother. There was nothing grovelling about Mary ; clearly she believed that honest work was honourable and that keeping out of debt and attending confession regularly were of great importance. Her one obsession was that her good-looking daughter, Annie, should have advantages she had never known. Annie must get ahead in the world. She must be somebody. I think if it would have helped Annie's career, Mary Scanlon, devout Catholic that she was, would have done away with herself.

Annie was not ashamed of her mother, yet whenever Mary Scanlon came, just before supper-time, into the parlour where

Annie and I were making maps or working out some problem in mathematics, Annie would stiffen a little and a hard look would come into her eyes. It wasn't directed at her mother or even at me. It came from something that happened inside Annie herself. She was afraid that I would be too polite to her mother or patronize her. Sometimes it seemed to me that she was simply a mass of exposed nerves. Behind it, of course, lay the whole mesh of small-town class consciousness. Maybe it would have been better if I had never come down into the Flats at all. Maybe Annie would have suffered less.

There was never even the suggestion of love-making between us, not even any adolescent fumbling. I never kissed her, and although at times the accidental touch of our hands would cause me to blush and feel warm and confused, I know that on Annie's side it was no more than accidental. I don't believe she ever thought of me as a man or even a boy. The thing that existed between us was really the aching friendship of two children who were unhappy misfits in the world in which they found themselves.

Pete Scanlon, Annie's father, was something else. She was ashamed of him, perhaps rightly, not because he was poor and could scarcely read or write, nor because after losing one leg as a brakeman under a train while he was drunk, he was given the humble job of gate crossing-keeper which he also lost for the same reason, but because he was a drunkard and dirty despite anything Mary Scanlon could do to keep him clean. Pete was really something to be ashamed of, especially when, on his day off, he would sometimes bang upon the door and come cursing and swearing into the room saying, " Ah ! The little love-birds are doing their jography again. Sure, Davy, if you get my Annie in trouble you'll have to marry her even if you do live up on the hill."

Pete was awful. Both of us suffered inside, when he came bursting into the room, as if somebody turned a knife in our vitals. Once Mary Scanlon came in at the same time and when Pete began to shout, she said savagely, " Shut your bloody old trap or I'll bash it in for you. Sure and you ought to be ashamed of yourself embarrassing your own flesh and blood daughter before a fine young man like Davy Sorrell." She re-enforced her words with a brandish of the bottle of cleaning fluid she carried, and Pete went out of the room meek as a lamb, to leave us in peace.   But the evening was spoiled and quickly I took up my hat and went home.   It was the kindest thing I could do for Annie.

Through the better part of a whole year the curious friendship between the two of us grew and deepened.   There was no discussion of it between us, no recognition of it.   When we were together we both lived beyond the borders of Lewisburg in another world in which we were both clever and triumphant and desirable.   In the clean parlour of Mary Scanlon's neat little house, the whole pageant of history went by, with Annie and me playing great rôles.   Then one day I had a sudden shock ; I found that Annie's taste in non-history books was lurid.

I was myself a literary snob and I found that Annie was a passionate reader of the works of Ouida and other such authors. She kept the books hidden away in her room.   At the time I was shocked, for it seemed to me that a girl who was so clever at mathematics and languages should have better taste in literature.   Now I know that mathematics and appreciation of art rarely go together, although mathematics in itself is a great, exact and beautiful art.   And I know that Annie liked Ouida not because she thought it good literature but because in the pages she lived a romantic life among impossibly handsome men and passionate women, a world which never existed on land or sea or in the sky, but which was the antithesis of all that Lewisburg and the Flats represented.   It was, in a way, the kind of world which she found long afterwards in a decaying Europe.   She was aware of my snobbery and never talked about the books.

And then, at the end of the third year of High School, the intimacy was broken up.   One reason was that Annie had had enough of High School, and as she grew older she realized that her mother's dream for her future was a sad, romantic thing never to be realized.   She knew suddenly that her mother, and much less her father, could never really help her.   She knew what it was she wanted, and also knew that she would never get it save through her own efforts.   She had the shrewdness which comes to intelligent people out of harsh experience with life.   So she did not go back to High School.   She left and went to Andrews Business College in the Masonic Temple Building to become a stenographer and learn accountancy.   She was

A.B.—B   [33]

happier there, because she was on her own. In a business college there wasn't any clannishness, and the other girls were poor and went there to learn a means of supporting themselves. She never heard any of them talk about going to Vassar or Wellesley. She never saw anyone there whose house was cleaned by her mother.

But there was another element that came between us. It was the boy called Tom Harrigan.

I don't know why she and Tom Harrigan never got together in High School; perhaps because she made no effort to be friendly and turned her back on every gesture or indication of friendship. She always was afraid of people being kind to her. But it wasn't altogether that.

I can't remember that during the three years Tom showed any awareness of her presence. He wasn't very much interested in girls. He was pretty good in his classes and very good at sports. He was the best half-back the football team ever had; he played as well in the basketball and baseball teams, and established a high jump record for high schools on the track team. All this, with a little studying on the side, didn't leave him much time for girls.

He was as good-looking a boy as I have ever seen—the Irish kind with black curly hair and blue eyes and high colour, with big heavy shoulders and long straight legs. There wasn't anything complicated about him; that was one reason why he was so good an athlete. I envied him the simplicity of his approach to life, the directness with which he attacked every-thing that interested him, and his utter absorption in whatever he was doing. I suppose he fell in love the same way he did everything else. He knew what it was all about without being told. He knew with the sure instinct of a young male animal what it was that he wanted and went for it. It was all very simple, and straightforward, and glowing with the health which seemed to envelop him in a kind of radiance.

People liked Tom, I think because it made them feel good just to be near him. Boys liked him, and at that age some of them worshipped him to the point of adoration. They quoted what he said and dressed like him. And the girls fell in love with him, although he never paid much attention to them beyond making a joke or giving them a slap now and then on the rump. No other boy in school would have dared such a boldness with the respectable girls from the big houses on Centre Avenue. From Tom they didn't seem to mind it ; on the contrary, they would giggle and bridle and flush and display surprising signs of sex, although as a rule the existence of sex was hardly admitted in their world. Looking back, I suspect that if he had chosen to, he could have seduced most of them as easily as he seduced Annie. He just wasn't interested in them and with Annie he fell in love.

I knew him very well, because, like everybody else, I fell for him. At that age he was everything I wanted to be— handsome, reckless, male, good at everything, with plenty of money to spend. I wasn't very much any of these things, and in a curious psychological way I tried to identify myself with him in a hundred small ways. One was to do his history and composition papers for him. I was awfully good at these things and the result was that he got good marks and had a lot more time for football and track work. We liked each other, I suppose, because in a way we complemented each other. The very core of his attraction was a kind of healthy animal magnetism.

That night in London, as I walked back to the hotel from Haddonfield House, the memory of Tom Harrigan returned to me with great vividness, almost as if he had joined me in the darkness and was walking at my side. It seemed to me that he was the most attractive man, young or old, I had ever known —the kind who should never die because of the brightness they bring into the world. And then, pushing the idea a little further, it occurred to me that perhaps it was better in the long run that he had died young while he still had that bright- ness. Perhaps, although his death did something destructive to Anna, it was better for her sake as well.

I tried to imagine what would have happened if he had gone on living, and it seemed to me inevitable that presently he would have begun to grow heavy and a little coarse, and that after a time a certain aimlessness and boredom would have come into his life simply because he was no longer young ; and a little later he would have taken to drink and all that was bright and attractive would have become dulled and tarnished. I believed this because I was by then old enough to have seen this pattern repeated again and again with boys like Tom, who had been bright and splendid when they were young and who turned into something drunken and despairing at middle age.

There seemed, after all, to be some handicap in being born with everything, with too much. To get ahead, to have a rich life of accomplishment and satisfaction, there had to be obstacles and bitterness and resentments. I began thinking over the successful and great people I had known out of my own life, and out of all those people I could not think of one who had started off life with the good fortune and equipment of Tom Harrigan. Each one of them had been ugly, or poor, or possessed of a physical handicap or some odd twist of psychology. It was as if mankind needed obstacles to drive it on. When I was seventeen I wanted to be like Tom Harrigan, to *be* Tom Harrigan more than anything in the world; at thirty-five, as I walked along Park Lane coming from Anna's enormously successful party, I was aware that the desire was dead.

The odd thing was that Annie, as a girl, had had the same good looks and brightness as Tom, that same quality which would have drawn people to her if she had permitted it. But with her there were obstacles. She was poor. Her mother was the charwoman, her father a drunken, Irish crossing-keeper with a wooden leg. She lived in the Flats. She had an inflexible pride which would accept nothing, not even kindness or friendship, from people whom she suspected of patronizing her, and she suspected everyone.

I do not know why Tom, who had never noticed her in all the years she was in the same class with him, suddenly became aware of her once she was no longer there. Perhaps it was because he himself was older, or because, when she put her hair up and went to business college, she seemed another person. Perhaps it was simply because he had come to the age where girls became important to him. He was the kind to whom women would always be a necessity. In any case I discovered one day that they were seeing each other and that this was the reason why he had stopped going out in the evenings with the rest of the boys.

Annie, now that she had left High School, seemed to be settling into the rôle suggested by her appearance and the circumstances of her life. Sometimes you saw Tom and her out together in an ice-cream parlour or at a roadhouse in one of the near-by villages. I think her mother was pleased because Tom's father was rich and he was Irish and a Catholic, and he didn't have the Centre Avenue background which could never accept Annie. I don't know what Tom's parents thought in the beginning. Perhaps they knew nothing about it. Annie couldn't bring him to her own house for fear that her father might come in drunk at any time and make a scene. And they never went to the Harrigans' showy new house. She told me that she had never seen the inside of it. They had to meet at movies or ice-cream parlours, or go on long drives when Tom could get his father's car.

I didn't know then how far the affair went, although I suspected that Tom was not the type to go about courting indefinitely in the Centre Avenue manner, holding hands and getting no more than a kiss now and then ; and so far as Annie was concerned, I knew that in the Flats there weren't many conventions or moral restraints. Down there girls didn't usually get married until they were pregnant and sometimes not even then. There was one thing very clear—that Tom was as much absorbed in the adventure with Annie as he had always been in anything he undertook. Once the thing started going, his other interests faded out. He became a lackadaisical athlete, despite his natural animal strength and health. His record in school went down and down. There was only Annie. In an odd way he was never adolescent like the other fellows. He never went through the pimply stage, nor calf love, nor sighing and writing poetry. He was a boy and then all at once, when he fell in love with Annie, he was a man, unmistakably a man, with a new seriousness and a new kind of authority.

I know now that what happened between the two of them was a remarkably beautiful thing, a kind of model of what love should be between two young people—simple, natural, healthy and fine. At first Annie was interested because she knew that the news of the affair would irritate all the girls from Centre Avenue. At first she flaunted Tom's attentions, but presently she was as much in love as Tom, and after that she became as secret about the whole thing as he himself wanted to be. This was not because he was ashamed of her background ; he never gave a damn about a thing like that. It was because this being in love was a secret thing they wanted to keep to themselves.

It went on like that for more than a year, and in the autumn Tom went away to Notre Dame to college. But he didn't stay there. He came back secretly on week-ends to Summerstown across the river and she went over there to meet him. People had expected him to be a great Notre Dame football star, but nothing like that happened. He wasn't even good enough to get into the team and after he took to disappearing over week-ends, he was thrown out altogether.

In a way, their week-end meetings across the river were the happiest times in all their lives together. They were young and in love, and nothing else mattered. Annie said that he was always a perfect lover from the very beginning, just as he was a perfect athlete or a perfect student when he chose to be. Nothing mattered to them in those days but the happiness of being together. The rest of the world ceased to exist. They had what few people ever know, a perfect happiness that was as spiritual as it was physical.

In the spring Annie discovered that she was going to have a baby. She wasn't frightened but only puzzled about what she should do. She knew that it was impossible to go to her own mother, who would only reproach her bitterly and view the whole thing as a disaster and the end of all her ambitions for her daughter. Her mother would make a scandal or try to force Tom to marry her. It was one of those curious relationships in which a mother whose whole life had been one of bitter defeat sought insanely to use her daughter as compensation. But Annie's own pride as an individual came into the whole thing and so she saw it as something which concerned herself and Tom alone.

When she told him, he was not puzzled at all. He said quite simply with a curious mature wisdom, " We'll get married. After all, that's why we love each other. That's the way things are. That's why people fall in love—to have babies. That's the way it was meant to be."

When Annie told me this, years later, the tears came into her eyes.

Tom knew what it meant—that he would have to give up college, that very likely his father and mother would disown him, that he would have to go to work at any job he could find. There were many things he had not told her, because he had not wanted to hurt her. The most important was that his parents had found out what was going on and tried to stop it ; they had told him that if ever he married that " charwoman's daughter " he could never bring her into their house, that they would never see her, and that he could expect no money from them.

[38]

So Annie once more found herself brought up against all the barriers of that little world of Lewisburg, only this time there was an element involved that was almost more defeating than the caste feeling of Protestant Centre Avenue. It was the feeling of superiority of successful " lace curtain " Irish over " shanty " Irish. In all the world there is no snobbery greater than that.

There was no reconciling Tom's parents to the marriage. They had other children. They could do without Tom for a time. His father said to him, " You'll find out your mistake soon enough and want to get out of it." And his mother said, " You can't marry that kind of a girl. You'll soon find out what she is. She trapped you into it. Only remember one thing. Once you're married you're married. Good Catholics don't get divorced."

Tom didn't argue with them. That same night he and Annie went across the river to Summerstown and were married, not in the church but by a Justice of the Peace. They had between them but a few dollars. Before they went away Tom came by the house and told me. I was the only person in town he bothered to tell and I was flattered.

I still am flattered, but the memory troubled me when Anna gave me the blank look devoid of all recognition at the top of the stairs in Haddonfield House. I wanted to say, " But don't you remember that when Tom and you ran away across the river to be married I was the only one in the whole town he told about it ? "

But that wasn't the kind of thing you could say under the circumstances, and I was certain, considering what Anna had become, that she didn't care any longer about the memory of Tom, and did not even want to be reminded of him. The hard, worldly Anna who stood at the top of the stairs had scarcely any physical resemblance to the full-breasted, voluptuous girl who crossed the river that night with Tom. Only the pride which still remained seemed to bring the two together.

Tom got himself a job as an automobile salesman in Pittsburgh and they rented a flat and about December the baby, a boy, was born. Tom was only twenty and Annie was nineteen. They were perfectly happy and Tom did very well from the start. He was the kind of person who didn't have to work hard to persuade anybody to buy anything. If he told somebody a certain car was a good car, they believed it was the best car in the world and bought it at once. I think they liked to buy things from Tom, just to please him. There were many people, miserable and complicated and frustrated people, who got a sense of strength and confidence simply out of talking to him. None of them, certainly not myself, was ever aware that with Tom as with others like him, the shallowness, the superficiality were completely obscured by a kind of physical radiance.

Not very long after the baby was born his family began trying to get him away from Anna. They missed him a great deal more than they had believed possible. They began writing to him, and an older brother came to Pittsburgh; but Tom wouldn't answer the letters and wouldn't talk to his brother. For about a year the family gave up the attempt and then began again with no more success than before; at last one of them, Annie never knew which one it was, sent Tom a telegram which read : " Father critically ill. Come at once."

He came home from the office, kissed the baby and Annie good-bye and set off for Lewisburg. She never saw him alive again. Near Marietta the speeding car skidded into a truck on the icy road and Tom was killed.

He was buried in Lewisburg and Annie went to the funeral, but she never spoke to any of his family. Worst of all, she discovered that the father had never really been critically ill at all. It was a winter of influenza and he, like half the town, had caught it. The whole thing had been a trick.

She stayed overnight with her parents and then went back to Pittsburgh and the baby. She got herself a job, and left the baby at a day nursery. There he caught measles which turned into pneumonia, and a little less than a year after Tom's death the baby died too.

Annie Harrigan was not quite twenty-two years old and alone in the world once more, more alone than she had ever been even in the days when she went to High School in Lewisburg. I met her in the street the day she came back from the funeral of the baby. Something had happened to her eyes. They were like stone, as if there were no more tears in them.

We talked for a moment about nothing at all, never speaking either of Tom or the baby, and in the end she said abruptly and apropos of nothing, " Some day I'll get even with Lewisburg. You wait and see, some day I'll show Lewisburg ! "

Then she went away and I never saw her again until years later, in the lobby of the Ritz, in New York. A handsome woman and an elderly man came towards me and as they passed I only noticed that the woman was handsome and beautifully dressed. A dozen steps away I thought, " That is someone I know." And without thinking I turned and looked back. At the same moment the woman turned to look at me. Our glances met and she smiled and then I thought, " That looks like Annie Scanlon but it couldn't be." I smiled back at her and she spoke to the man and they both came towards me. I saw then that the woman *was* Annie. She looked scarcely any older, but in her eyes there was still that look of stone.

The man she introduced as her husband. " Mr. Bolton," she said, but the name didn't mean anything.

We had cocktails together and Annie asked me about my life. I told her that I had done well and had just returned from China, where I had been a correspondent. I suggested that we should have dinner together the next night, but the husband said they were leaving the next day for Detroit and there wasn't anything to be done about it.

" I live there now," she said.

She did not seem happy or unhappy. She looked very well and still had the radiant look of health and vitality, but there was a deadness of the spirit about her as if she had no very great interest in anything. Only once, when I mentioned Lewisburg, saying I hadn't been back there for a long time, did any life come into her face and then the look was only one of bitterness.

" Both my parents are dead," she said. " I haven't been back for a long time. Lewisburg is dead too, so far as I am concerned."

Then I remembered the remark about " showing Lewisburg." I thought, " She has done it, it seems. She has done very well. Her husband must have a great deal of money." The sable coat, the gown, the diamonds were all evidence of that. Although I may have imagined it, it seemed to me that these outward symbols of success gave her a feeling of satisfaction. But I still did not really know Annie or her insatiable ambition.

While we sat there I studied the husband, speculating on how she had met him and how the marriage had come about. He was a heavy, rather nice-looking man, the self-made type, I decided, perhaps sixty to sixty-five years old. Very likely she had been his secretary. Probably he had married in a final flare-up of desire when even a man in his position no longer thinks of such things as caste or background or wealth, knowing of how little value these things are in comparison to the greater thing he desired. It was clear that she made him happy, and equally clear that happiness of the sort he had expected was no longer of any consequence to her. She was beyond happiness or unhappiness. As she lifted her cocktail I noted the great size of the diamond and the emerald on her fingers.

" Yes," I thought, " she is making him very happy indeed."

But even then it did not occur to me that this Mr. Bolton could be *the* Mr. Bolton whose inventions and business skill had made him one of the richest men in America ; perhaps because it was almost impossible to connect Annie Scanlon, whose mother had been the charwoman from the Flats, with so much success.

They left after half an hour to dine and go to the theatre. I had the impression that Bolton didn't like me or the revival of old intimacies between Anna and me, that it made him feel an outsider, or perhaps that it reminded him of her humble origin.

I did not discover until long afterwards that I had guessed the story of the marriage. It was almost exactly as I had speculated. I did not discover that her husband was *the* Mr. Bolton until the first summer she came to London. By that time he was dead and she was one of the richest women in the world.

But even then she hadn't " shown Lewisburg." She had money, almost incredible amounts of it, invested in tax-exempt securities, but this in a way was only the beginning of what she wanted. With all the money she existed in a kind of luxurious void.

She had set out to show Lewisburg, but the curious thing was that Lewisburg, if it thought of her at all, wished her luck. Mary the charwoman was dead, and her pretty daughter was nearly forgotten. But the thing which drove Annie Scanlon was still alive, burning inside her, driving her on. Perhaps it would drive her on until the grave. Perhaps it would have but for what happened in France.

After the night of the party at Haddonfield House I went off again to the Continent on a trip which included Vienna, Moscow, Stockholm, Berlin, Rome, ending up finally in Paris in October. Wherever I went, save Moscow, I found the world disintegrating and rushing towards disaster. It was a world dominated by too many intriguers, by too many small people, a world lost for lack of decency and leadership, with scarcely a statesman in it. In Vienna there was a whole world tawdry and pathetic; Vienna was like an old whore who had once been very pretty. In Berlin there was a semblance of order and plan, but a plan that was terrifying in the madness of its concentration upon destruction, a plan destined, I felt, to succeed for a while, not only because elsewhere there was only folly and weakness and disintegration to oppose it, but because even in the countries which the plan was designed to destroy there were men like Bonnet and Schuschnigg, Chamberlain and Ciano who, either from self-interest or stupidity, were bent upon helping Berlin.

In France the people were on the brink of revolt against the corruption and intrigue of their own government.

But Rome was worst of all. The Dictator kept half a dozen more or less professional mistresses. Ciano, the foreign minister, was one of a dozen amateurs whom one met night after night at dinners where gambling until dawn was the great diversion. The Grand and the Excelsior were filled with Russians, French, Germans, English, Austrians, Spanish, none of them up to any good, and rich Americans there simply for the enjoyment of this picture of decay and disaster. Yet about it all there was the curious atmosphere not of a world capital, but of a provincial town riddled with gossip and intrigue and envy. One felt that every evening the Queen, the Princess Colonna and Mrs. Mussolini must go down to the station to see the trains go through.

It was in Rome that I again crossed the trail of Anna. She had had a great success. Everyone knew her. The British Ambassador, urged no doubt from far-off London by Lady Haddonfield, had given a dinner in her honour the day after her arrival. From then on she had gone everywhere, to the great balls given by people like the Colonnas and the Rospigliosis and the Peccis, to the small dinners where Ciano and Edda Mussolini (la petroleuse, as the French Embassy called her) played backgammon and poker for huge stakes with the Roman fast set.

One or two people saw through Anna and laughed at her or were bitter about the vulgar American woman who bought whatever she wanted. But with most of them she was a success. There was nothing spectacular about her. She did not drink,

perhaps because she found all the excitement she needed elsewhere in her own perpetual astonishment at the sight of Annie,
the charwoman's daughter, frequenting the lofty company of
Mussolini (himself the son of an honest blacksmith) and his
daughter (who was not even legitimatized until she was a grown
woman) and a Foreign Minister (who in reality was a kind of
gigolo) and a Princess (who was the daughter of a rich Syrian
rug merchant) and a Papal count who was a conventional New
Yorker, and a great many men and women with names that were
brilliant at the time of the Renaissance and now lived any way
they could. It was a fine dazzling background for Anna and
one in which it was very easy to go as far as you liked along
the path she had chosen for herself, so long as you were very
rich, or very clever, or very unscrupulous. Rome was the mad
carnival of Europe at its worst.

Oddly enough, you heard no scandal about Anna, save what
was regarded as a scandal in that special world—the fact that
a handsome woman of thirty-five had no lover, not even a
semblance of one. She lived in the Sodom and Gomorrah
of a fashionable hotel as she lived in Haddonfield House in
London, in utter chastity, companioned only by the servants
and Miss Godwin.

I confess that this aspect of her life rather astonished me, for
I could not reconcile it with the memories of the full-blooded,
rather voluptuous girl who had sat across the aisle from me in
the Lewisburg High School. By all the rules I knew, this purity
of behaviour was simply not in keeping with Anna's type. It
was natural that she had already had offers of marriage. No
woman with that much money could have gone long in Europe
without them, even if she had been as ugly as the three-headed
Cerberus, which Anna certainly was not. But none of these
offers seemed to come to anything.

Miss Godwin keeps cropping up in the story and I suppose
now is as good a time as any to tell about her.

I have already described her at the party in Haddonfield
House. She went wherever Anna went and it is important to
the story to remember that all through the triumphs, among
all the new people Anna came to know, Miss Godwin remained
her greatest friend, perhaps her only real friend, who sought
nothing at all from her, who worked for a salary and really
gave far more than any salary could buy. For she gave Anna

dignity and protected her from herself and her own ignorance and folly, as well as from those who sought to swindle her or impose upon her.

It was the secretary, Miss Godwin, who knew all the answers. Beneath the old-fashioned, dignified exterior, there lay tragedy and years of anxiety and experience. Once, a very long time before, she had been rich, and once she had lived in a Europe very different from the one Anna knew—the Europe of Edward VII. Miss Godwin knew exactly what people like a Lady Haddonfield or a Countess Ciano were worth. She knew when they had risen from nothing, learning nothing on the way, and she knew when, born to every advantage, they threw them all away and deteriorated to the level of trollops and swindlers. In a way it was as if she had been sent by God to Anna on the morning she called at the Ritz in New York, at the suggestion of an acquaintance who knew that a certain rich Mrs. Bolton was looking for a travelling companion and secretary.

Behind Miss Godwin, as she stood that morning in the doorway of Anna's sitting-room, there was a dead fiancé, killed forty years earlier in an accident a week before the wedding was to have occurred, a fiancé whom she never had known as a lover and whom she was never able to forget. Behind her lay the awful shadow of genteel poverty which had returned again as the ill winds of the depression blew across America. In a way her life had been the reverse of Anna's. She had begun it as the pretty daughter of a rich man, and as she stood in the doorway of Anna's apartment in the New York Ritz she faced the end of her life in the bitterest of poverty. A little while before—only three or four years—she had made a good living arranging debutante parties for the daughters of rich men; providing lists of eligible and correct young men who might be invited; planning showy, extravagant weddings; doing floral decorations. Miss Godwin was known for her cultivation and good taste.

And then one morning there were no more very rich men but only men terrified by the future, and no more great "coming out" parties, no more showy weddings, no more vast orders for flowers. And on the same morning Miss Godwin discovered that her "nest egg," all that she had counted on to make her comfortable in her old age, was gone too, and at sixty she was forced to go out and look for a job.

[45]

That was how she came to Anna at the Ritz.

It seemed to be all right from the beginning, for after they had talked for a little while, Miss Godwin discovered that Anna too had been hurt, how she did not know, but the signs of the hurt were there in her voice and eyes.

Miss Godwin, sitting a little on the edge of a gilt Ritz chair, trembling inside herself, very proud and very frightened and a little tired, explained what she knew and what she was able to do and finished by asking, " What exactly is it you would want of me, Mrs. Bolton ? "

The colour came into Anna's face and she turned away towards the window. Then she said, " I've had an odd life, Miss Godwin. I've never been able to do what I wanted to do or be what I wanted to be. I can't go into the reasons—at least not unless I know someone very well and I've never known anyone well enough yet to talk about it."

That was as near as she ever came to telling Miss Godwin about her life with Ezra Bolton. Afterwards, bit by bit, Miss Godwin learned the story of Tom from me, but the life with Ezra Bolton remained largely a blank except that she knew he had been rich, eccentric and jealous. It was as if, in her worst moments, Anna was more ashamed of the Ezra Bolton episode than she was of her origin on the wrong side of the tracks in Lewisburg. It may have been because the years with her second husband were a kind of desert in which nothing at all happened, in which she herself had had no existence at all.

A little way outside Detroit Ezra Bolton had built for his first wife, in the early days of his affluence, a monstrous stone house, more like a feudal castle than a home. He had furnished it according to the tastes of his first wife, a girl he had married while he still operated a bicycle shop in Van Wert, Ohio. It was a house filled with Neapolitan statuary, with conservatories and turrets and vast red-carpeted stairways. Nor had it ever really been lived in, for the first wife had been an invalid for twenty years before she died. The vast dining-room had never echoed to the sound of voices, the great halls saw only servants and Bolton himself and two or three rather dreary women who visited the wife. It was a kind of rich and vulgar tomb, a monument to the epoch when Detroit was a raw town owned mostly by sudden millionaires.

It was here that Bolton brought his second bride and here she lived until he died, without enough interest even to change the decorations. By the time Bolton married Annie, he had become an eccentric. He saw only the men with whom he did business, and even these he never brought to his house. Perhaps this was because, during the long dreary period of his first wife's illness, he had lost the habit, or perhaps because, with an elderly man's passion for a young, good-looking wife, he lived in terror that she might find some other man more attractive. Anna said she didn't know and that it may have been a little of both. In any case she rarely saw anyone save the servants and her husband unless there was an accidental meeting such as that I had with them in the New York Ritz.

He was a kind and gentle man, almost humble in his adoration, and pathetically so in his occasional love-making. " It was always," Anna said, " as if he apologized to me for being a nuisance. I never tried to make him believe that I loved him. I was fond of him and he was very good to me in his strange way. I tried to make him understand the affection I felt for him. But there was something deformed about him emotionally. Perhaps it was because during the best years of his life he had had an invalid, complaining wife. I think he was faithful to her all that time. At first when I came to work for him, he was afraid of me. Even when I took his dictation and later when I got to be a kind of executive assistant, he would always leave the office door ajar when I was with him. I never did the faintest thing to attract him. You see, at that time, there was really only Tom in my life. There couldn't have been any other man—much less a man so much older than myself. There wasn't anyone, young or old, who could have taken Tom's place. I only wanted to get ahead by my brains and be one of those successful business women executives."

She told me all of this long afterwards in the villa in Algiers. I doubt that she ever told anyone else.

She said, " And then one evening just as he was leaving the office he said to me suddenly, ' Mrs. Harrigan, I would like to marry you.' I had no answer because I hadn't even suspected any interest. I had always thought he was afraid of me. I told him I would have to think it over and thanked him, almost formally. Like most inventors and people who work with machinery, there was something very simple about him, something almost childlike. I couldn't imagine hurting him.

"He didn't press me. I thought it over for nearly a week and at last one evening I said simply, 'I've been thinking over what you asked me, Mr. Bolton. I think I'd like to accept.' It seemed to me a wise thing to do. You see, I never thought of marrying or ever falling in love again, and quite coldly I considered what it all meant. He was a nice man and he had more money than most people ever dream of. I knew that he was alone in the world and that very likely he would die before me and that most of the money would be mine, and then I could do all the things I had dreamed about even long ago when you used to walk home from school with me and we sat in the parlour." As she told me this she smiled, "And I thought too that I would be showing Lewisburg.

"And so we were married and he wanted me to give up working. He was an old-fashioned man. He said he couldn't think of me as a wife if I went to work with him in the mornings. So I gave in to him and went to live in that huge awful house. It didn't seem so awful to me then. It just seemed enormously and frighteningly rich. And I had a vague ambitious plan in the back of my head to learn more, to educate myself. I don't think I knew very clearly what I wanted. I only thought that a life like that would give me time to read books I'd never had time to read or even find, and I wanted to learn to speak French and German and Italian.

"That was just the way it worked out. It was like going back to school again. I always liked school. The only thing I missed in that strange life was competition. There wasn't anyone in that big house I could show off to. We never went anywhere but to a theatre or a movie. He loved that and for me it broke up the monotony. In all that time I never really met anyone except casually in restaurants and hotel lobbies, the way I met you that night in the Ritz. I learned a lot and got to speak French and Italian pretty well. And then one morning, one of the maids came to my room and said Mr. Bolton didn't answer when she knocked on his door. He was dead and when they opened his will, Dave, I found that I, Annie Scanlon, had an income of about a million dollars a year."

She sighed and said, "It was a curious experience—as if four years were missing from my life—four years in which nothing had happened at all but what I had learned out of books. I was suddenly alone in the world with about a million dollars a year and a lot of vague ambitions."

That is very briefly what she told me a long time afterwards. That day in the New York Ritz, while Miss Godwin sat a little forward on the gold chair wondering where she would find money for next morning's breakfast, Anna only said, explaining to Miss Godwin as best she could, " I feel as if I was born to be somebody—somebody I've never been yet. It's as if one side of me had never grown up, as if I was a little deformed inside me. I want to know all kinds of people. I don't really know anybody. I want to go everywhere and see everything." She hesitated again. "I want to grow up to my full size. I want to get rid of a lot of things—scars, I guess you might call them—before it's too late. I have money—so much money I can't possibly spend it all. I am absolutely free. I have no relatives even. What I want is someone to help me—to tell me what to do, to tell me when I'm being a fool, to keep me from being laughed at."

She rose and crossed the room and stood looking out of the window, into Madison Avenue. After a moment she said, " I think that's about as far as I can go in explaining." Then she turned and asked, " Is it far enough for you to understand ? "

Miss Godwin had been watching her all the time, studying her clothes, the way she walked, her voice and the way she spoke, the way her hair was dressed, and with her knowledge of the world she noticed many things—that this strange young woman was handsome, that she had a pleasant voice, that she was intelligent and had natural taste, that there was something pathetic about her. She divined too that Anna could tell the things she had told only to a perfect stranger like Miss Godwin but never to anyone she knew at all.

Miss Godwin said, " I think so. I think perhaps I could be of service. I don't know. We shall have to make a try of it." You must remember too that Miss Godwin was desperate.

And so the strange interview ended, Miss Godwin going back to her flat feeling happier about the arrangement than she had ever expected to feel. She had gone to the Ritz prepared to accept almost any terms and to find some tyrannical middle-aged or elderly woman awaiting her, for whom she would have to work because she was desperate. And instead she found a kind of attractive mystery which aroused her curiosity and interest to a degree she had not thought possible at her age. She had gone to the Ritz feeling that her life was finished and that what remained of it would be given over to a dreary servitude as companion and secretary to some dreadful old woman. And now she had discovered the possibility of a whole new life, lived through someone else, a woman scarcely more than half her age—a life which had up to now been denied her. She kept her fingers crossed, but it was a little like being born again at the age of sixty.

It was Miss Godwin who decided that they were to go to Europe. Knowing the world, she knew that it would be much easier to attempt there what Anna wanted than it would ever be in America. In the first place the show itself was better and in the second place, odd as it seemed, people in Europe cared less what you were or what you had been in the past than in America. They asked only that you be rich, or famous, or eccentric, or notorious. Miss Godwin was aware that somewhere in Anna's background there was a mystery, although she had no idea what it was—a mystery of which Mrs. Bolton was ashamed. In Europe no one would know about it ; nor would anyone be too curious concerning the past.

So they went to London and for the first season lived quietly at Claridge's, meeting casually some of the Edwardian relics whom Miss Godwin had known well enough long ago, people of irreproachable background and great position. Through these people Anna met others and by the end of several months she and Miss Godwin were well enough established to consider undertaking a real campaign. Between seasons they travelled, spending a lot of time in Paris. It was in the third season that I saw Miss Godwin for the first time and took Anna's hand as she stood at the top of the stairs in Haddonfield House without any sign of recognition in her eyes. Even then Miss Godwin did not know more than a few details concerning her past. She only knew that Anna was a very good student and that she had been twice married, the second time to a very rich man, in his way an eccentric, who was jealous of her and gave her everything save the companionship of other people.

" It was," said Miss Godwin afterwards, " like dealing with a case of arrested development. There were so many things to which Anna reacted in a perfectly childish way. It was like a case of infantilism in which the victim liked everything which glittered and placed a value upon all the showy things—like a child suddenly confronted by a table filled with sweets, intent only on stuffing herself with them all as rapidly as possible."

Most of the time Anna and Miss Godwin got on very well together and they became very fond of each other. But there were times when the relationship became difficult and there were times when Anna seemed swept away beyond the borders of any reality. She would become self-hypnotized by pleasure at the list of a dance which included the names of a dozen notorious or titled people, or entranced by the sight of her name in the gossip columns along with those of all the fast, notorious or famous people, the cabinet ministers, the actresses. She wanted only the most wonderful jewels and the most fantastic furs. There were times when to Miss Godwin she must have seemed a monster.

But Miss Godwin was fond of her as one is fond of a child and she knew that she herself was very well off and had nothing to complain of. And the sight of a Europe on the verge of destruction held an evil fascination for her. Of course what she did not know was that every time Anna gave a dinner, or took a handsome house, or bought a wonderful jewel or a fur coat, she was " showing Lewisburg "—the Lewisburg which probably never would know because she herself would never acknowledge it.

By the time I reached Rome they had already gone to Venice, where Anna took the Palazzo Cienferra for the late summer and autumn. That winter I was sent to India and from there to China and then back to Moscow and it was nearly two years before I crossed her path again.

In Anna's world nothing had changed very much. In England and France governments came and went but essentially they were all the same—blundering, stupid, corrupt or divided. Miss Godwin watched, fascinated and horrified, absorbed in the spectacle as she might be absorbed by a lurid melodrama.

On my return I decided that the time had come for a holiday, and went south to Monte Carlo, and there, in the Hôtel de Paris,

I found Anna and Miss Godwin. They were between places—Cannes, I think, and Biarritz—and they were not there long enough to take a house. Anna was really letting herself go, with a Rolls-Royce, a chauffeur, a maid and a second secretary who permitted Miss Godwin more time to look after flowers and invitations and parties. Anna was in the midst of that world which dazzled her, an accepted part of it, no longer simply a fabulously rich American curiosity. She had done it quickly, as if she, like all the others in that world, had been aware that the time was growing short and they must hurry.

Then, one afternoon as I was sitting on the terrace of the Casino watching the life of the tiny harbour below, Miss Godwin came across the terrace and sat down next to me. She looked tired and much older than when I had last seen her. For a time I sat there smoking and drinking in silence, now watching the harbour, now stealing a glance at Miss Godwin who sat with the finely cut profile towards me, apparently looking out across the Mediterranean but clearly seeing nothing at all. She was dressed in a rather old-fashioned dress of grey silk with a black hat.

After a little time my curiosity got the better of me, and turning towards her I said, " I beg your pardon. May I introduce myself ? I am David Sorrell. By profession I am a newspaper correspondent. We met for a moment in London a couple of years ago."

A startled, rather suspicious and hostile look came into her eyes and went away again, and she said surprisingly, " Yes, I remember. I'm very glad to know you."

I could see she thought for a moment that I was going to ask some favour. I suppose always being with Anna made her like that—always suspecting everyone of wanting something, money or invitations or assistance of some sort.

After a moment I asked, " Are you staying long in Monte Carlo ? "

" Only two days more. Then we go to Biarritz. Mrs. Bolton has taken Jean Patou's house there for September."

" Is she well ? "

" Yes . . . physically well."

It was a curious remark which I failed to understand. Then Miss Godwin turned her chair towards me abruptly and said, " Mr. Sorrell, I feel that we are both beating about the bush."

" Perhaps. Why do you think that ? "

She smiled a rather cold smile and then said, " I think we would both like to know what the other knows about Mrs. Bolton. I hope you don't believe I am saying this out of idle curiosity or because I wish to practise blackmail. The reasons are quite different—quite the contrary. I might as well tell you that Mrs. Bolton pointed you out to me the night of the party in London. She said to me, ' Miss Godwin, notice the man standing in the doorway. I used to know him very well. He's quite famous now.' Afterwards when I asked about you and heard your name, I knew at once that you were *The Times* correspondent. But she told me nothing more. At the time it seemed to me odd that she called my attention to you and then afterwards passed it off without explaining herself. I might as well tell you that when I came out on the terrace just now I noticed you and thought, ' That's someone I know from somewhere.' And then it came to me—where I had seen you and who you were. I might as well confess that I came over deliberately and sat down beside you, hoping in a way to pick you up."

She chuckled with more wickedness than I thought could be hidden behind so virginal and distinguished an exterior.

" I'm very glad you did. I was very fond of Anna once."

" A long time ago ? "

" We were seventeen or eighteen years old."

The answer gave her evident satisfaction. She gave me a quick glance.

" Then you could help me," she said, and repeated, " You mustn't think it is idle curiosity."

An idea occurred to me. I said, " Are you by any chance free for dinner to-night ? I'm just loafing here, doing whatever turns up."

" I *could* dine," she said, not giving in too quickly. " Mrs. Bolton is in Cannes. She's not expecting to see me."

It was settled then and there. We would dine in a small restaurant on the harbour, where we wouldn't be likely to see anyone we knew.

We had a cocktail and she said, " You must understand that I am very fond of Mrs. Bolton. I've been with her long enough to know her very well. I think I can say we are very good friends. That's why I'm worried. I want to do something to help her but I don't know how. I don't really know anything about her. Usually friends confide a little in each other. They tell things or things slip out. But nothing has ever slipped out of Mrs. Bolton. It's as if she had been born the day I met her. Beyond that I really know nothing at all except that she must have been very unhappy and that she is unhappy again."

I told her that I would be glad to do anything I could to help. We had another cocktail. It rather surprised me that she had a second one but it seemed to make it easier for her to talk.

"You see," she said, "I've never run across anyone who ever knew her except you . . . not one person. Considering how much we've been around, that seems rather extraordinary."

I smiled, "Maybe not so extraordinary as it might seem."

"Sometimes lately I've thought about writing to someone in Detroit to ask about her . . . you know Detroit was where she lived once."

"Yes, I know." I had a third cocktail and asked, "What is it that worries you about Anna?" And then I realized that we had both given up thinking about her as "Mrs. Bolton" and were speaking of her as "Anna."

She didn't answer at once and then she said, "Sometimes lately I think she is going mad. She goes faster and faster. She is more and more restless. At times it seems to me that she thinks she is a queen or an empress or something . . . that she believes she can do and have anything she wants—that money buys everything."

Miss Godwin looked away for a moment and sighed. Then she said, "She's too good for that kind of thing, Mr. Sorrell. She's very clever . . . she's learned to speak French and Italian perfectly. She's a very good business woman. She's kind and she's generous when she chooses to be, only she chooses to be more and more rarely. She doesn't trust anyone. She doesn't seem to believe that anyone can be decent or kind. There are times when she doesn't even trust me. You see, I can't help her because I don't know how. I don't know enough. I don't really know anything. Maybe you could tell me. Maybe you could help. She seems to go faster and faster. . . . It can't last much longer."

There was no doubt about the old lady's sincerity.

Out over the Mediterranean the sun was nearly down. The afternoon crowd was leaving the Casino and the terrace was filling with cocktailers.

I said, " I think we might go and dine. It's getting a little crowded here."

The restaurant was a place famous for its fish and wine on the *quai* overlooking the harbour. There were only two or three other people in it and they sat at a little distance from us. We dined well; Miss Godwin, despite her rather pinched, distinguished look, knew her food and liked it. Over the good dinner and the good wine we were very cosy and in a little while we seemed like old friends.

While we sat there, I told her the whole story of Lewisburg, of Tom, of his death and the death of the baby, and of how Anna had disappeared after that, just as I have told it earlier. I could tell her nothing of the Bolton interlude, for at that time I knew nothing of it. She did not interrupt me but listened passionately, forgetting her coffee until it grew quite cold. When I had finished with the chance meeting in the New York Ritz, she said, " I'm very glad I spoke to you. It makes it all much simpler. It makes it possible to understand a great deal more."

And then she told me her part of the story, beginning with the interview at the Ritz when she took the post of companion and secretary. Once or twice, as I listened, the thought occurred to me that we were living in an improbable world—two people like Miss Godwin and myself sitting in a waterfront restaurant in Monte Carlo discussing Annie Scanlon from the wrong side of the tracks, worrying about her, troubled about what was to become of her. And I thought, " There must be something better in Anna than appears on the surface—something which both of us *know* is there . . . which I have always known was there . . . else we shouldn't have taken the trouble to speak to each other in the beginning. We shouldn't care enough to be talking about her now."

Miss Godwin was saying, " The thing is how to get her back on the track . . . if something can't be done, the end will be terrible. Do you think there is anything you can do ?"

I shrugged my shoulders, " I think she would only resent me. She denied me in London. You say she is worse now than then ?"

" Sometimes," said Miss Godwin, " I think she may be taking something . . . drugs, I mean." And after a moment she added almost passionately, " You see. It's all wrong. She was meant to have a husband, a man she loved, and children. She wasn't made for all this. It's unnatural. It's perverted—living as she does, this wild, perfectly empty life. It would be much better if she had a lover who made a slave of her. It would be much better than this silly existence."

I looked at her, astonished at how much this remarkable spinster seemed to know. I said, "I don't know what to advise. It all goes back, I'm afraid, to the beginning—like someone who as a child was crippled for life."

I paid the bill and slowly we climbed the steps back to the Casino. It was a brilliant moonlight night and the whole hillside, with the Casino and villas, had an unreal and incredibly romantic look. Down below us on a great barge in the harbour, the evening revue had begun. Behind the barge there was a brilliant burst of fireworks. Rockets and bombs burst overhead and searchlights played on a tableau of naked women. It was fantastic—like the end of the world.

We stopped for a moment to watch, and beside me in the moonlight I heard Miss Godwin say, "I don't like it. It makes me sick inside."

I understood what she meant. Then I heard her murmuring, "It won't be long now."

We went to the Casino for a nightcap. Miss Godwin held her liquor remarkably well. Walking into the gambling rooms, we came upon Anna at the five-thousand franc table. She was absorbed in the game and gambling wildly, as if instead of desiring to win she was trying to throw money away.

Without a word, as if by common agreement, we stepped behind some palms to watch. There was very little chance of her discovering us. In any case, she seemed far too absorbed in the play to notice anything else.

She was dressed in black, wearing the same wonderful emeralds and diamonds I had seen in London. Her face looked thin and a little haggard and she wore too much make-up. Near her, apparently in the same party, stood one of the Greek syndicate of professional gamblers, the wife of a corrupt French cabinet minister, one of the Murats, and Chiappe, the Corsican Chief of Paris Police, who with his disreputable son-in-law, Carbuccia, the editor of *Gringoire*, were great figures in the political world of France.

There was something grisly about it all. It was so evident

that Anna was trying to throw away great sums of money as if she hated it or held it in contempt. But she only kept winning, pile after pile of five-thousand franc chips. She looked as if what Miss Godwin had said were true—that she was taking drugs or had gone a little mad.

At my side Miss Godwin said, "You see?"

"Yes." And I thought, "Annie Scanlon, Mary the charwoman's daughter, has come a long way." But I didn't know whether it was up hill or down. It was as if you could see the shadow of her worthless, drunken father just behind her.

Then we went away and walked up the moonlit hill to the Hotel de Paris. It was a beautiful night. Moscow and Berlin and Paris and Rome, and all that was going on there, seemed very far away.

As we climbed the steps of the hotel, Miss Godwin said, "It's been a very nice evening. I'm very grateful to you. What you told me makes all the difference." She sighed, "It seems such a waste. I don't think she's 'showing Lewisburg' any more. I think it's got beyond that."

"If you should ever want anything, you can reach me in the Paris office." I gave her my card with the address of *The Times* office. "I don't think my seeing her would do any good. It might only be unpleasant and make matters worse."

"I believe you," she said, "I only want to understand and help her. What you've told me makes everything easier."

In the hall of the hotel Miss Godwin thrust the card into her handbag. Without looking up she said, "You know I've never discovered but one thing out of her past. That was a photograph of a young man. I found it among her things one day. I'm sure it was Tom Harrigan, although she never told me. She only said, 'It's someone I knew a long time ago.'"

So it was like that. It wasn't over yet.

"Good-night," Miss Godwin said. "We shall probably be off to Biarritz to-morrow or Thursday." Then she hesitated for a moment and said, "It isn't just as if it were Anna alone. The whole world is going to pieces."

Then she walked to the lift and I went to the desk to ask for mail. There was a telegram from the Paris office. It read: *"Have tried to reach you by telephone all afternoon stop Chamberlain flying to Berchtesgaden stop Return at once."* I thought, "There's no stopping it now. God knows when it will end."

I was going towards the lift when a man's voice came from behind me. It said, "Hello, Sorrell. Will you have a nightcap?"

I turned and saw Von Kleist. He was smiling and held out his hand, and in the eyes there was a queer mocking look.

"Oh hello," I said, and then, "Thanks no. I've got to be off by the Blue Train early to-morrow." I was still holding the telegram in my hand and I thrust it towards him. "Did you know this?" I asked.

He took the telegram, looked through it and gave it back to me. "Yes," he said, "I knew it."

I repeated Miss Godwin's words, "It won't be long now."

He shrugged his shoulders. "I wouldn't say that. I think it means we'll have peace." Then he smiled, "After all, it's the second time the British have come to see *us* . . . that's a sign of something."

It was indeed a sign of something—something extremely dangerous to the whole world.

Then I left him and went to bed where I lay awake for a long time thinking, trying to piece things together. It was odd that Von Kleist had turned up in Monte Carlo at the same time as the Paris Chief of Police, the unspeakable Carbuccia, and all the others. It might mean a lot or it might mean nothing at all. In any case, Anna, without understanding any of it, was in very strange and bad company. I remembered suddenly the look of admiration in Von Kleist's eyes as he stood in the doorway of the ballroom at Haddonfield House watching her. Perhaps that was why Von Kleist was here in Monte Carlo. I thought, "She can't be as mad as that."

The rest of the story is Anna's, as nearly as possible as she told it to me.

The collapse of France caught her in Paris.

You couldn't really tell what was going on. For forty-eight hours there had been no announcement of any kind made over the radio, and the lack of all news was worse than bad news, for it gave rise to panic—creating rumours that began nowhere and presently died away into nothing, only to be replaced by new and more terrifying ones. In rumours there is far more terror than in the simple statement of facts, however bad they may be. You heard that the French had turned back the

Germans between Abbeville and Amiens and then you heard that the Germans were at Senlis and as far east as Meaux. You heard that Paris had been declared an open city and the next moment you heard that the Germans had threatened to bomb it into ruins unless the government capitulated at once. Twice all Paris heard the distant thunder of bombs dropped in the Boulevard Suchet on the edge of the Bois.

The real panic began about thirty-six hours before the end. The rich who had châteaux or houses in the country had already left, as had a few of the middle class and some of the working people who had relatives in the Charente or Auvergne or elsewhere. Otherwise the city was calm. Here and there a small shop put up its shutters indicating that the proprietor had closed up and left town. At night, the streets were dark save for occasional faint blue lights. People gathered in little groups and exchanged rumours. They bought newspapers but there was nothing in them but more rumours.

And then suddenly, without explanation, the panic occurred. People began leaving Paris by automobiles, by train, on foot pushing their belongings ahead of them on push-carts. More and more shutters went up. Even some of the small restaurants closed down. All day and long into the night the procession moved along the grey streets, along the Rue de Castiglione, named after a woman of another fantastic theatrical era, through the Place Vendôme before the Ritz, through the Rue Cambon and the Rue de la Paix, towards the Gare de l'Est and the Gare d'Orsay and the gates on the south and west. Even at night the Place Vendôme was filled with bicycles and push-carts, with automobiles fighting their way through the crowd.

But inside the Ritz life went on as usual, perhaps because the timid had already gone and those who remained could not believe that Paris would fall, or that their world could ever possibly collapse in panic and ruin and dust. Some of them waited, secretly, hopefully for the arrival of the Germans, like a few rich Frenchmen or Frenchwomen who stayed behind without panic because their arrangements had already been made and they were ready to welcome the enemy. They were there, without loyalty to anything on earth save money. There were a lot of them in Anna's world. Lately even she had become aware of them with a faint vague feeling of nausea and disbelief.

[59]

But more than anything else Madame Ritz herself gave stability to the whole establishment. There were many people who did not believe in her existence—that there could be a Madame Ritz—or they thought that if there had been she must long since be dead. Many of them had seen her, small white-haired, chic, with her two Pekinese at her heels, going quietly about the big hotel, never knowing that she was the widow of the great César Ritz, that she was in her own right a great woman.

She lived quietly in a comfortable suite of rooms beneath the mansard, surrounded by her Pekinese and countless canaries in cages, a woman full of wisdom and utterly without illusions. She had lived through two wars and now found the flood of a third swirling through the Place Vendôme and the Rue Cambon just beneath her windows.

She knew most of the great and spectacular and notorious people of her time and had been unimpressed by most of them. Tragedy lay in her background, with a husband, who had always been her partner, becoming ill and then dying, leaving all the responsibility upon her small, sturdy shoulders. For her, hotels were the most important things in the world ; she had helped to create the Savoy, the London Ritz, the London Carlton, the New York Ritz. People had paid her fortunes merely for the use of her name. Indeed her name had long since become an expressive word in the English language. But of all the great hotels, the Paris Ritz was the one she loved best. That was and would always be *the* Ritz, the creation of herself and her dead husband. Wars, revolutions might come and go, but nothing would disturb its perfection. Even during the riots of 6th February and the day of the famous General Strike, the restaurant of the Ritz, alone of all great Paris restaurants, remained open, doing business as usual. Inside its doors you would never have known that outside in the streets there was shooting and rioting and death.

Each day she made a round of the whole establishment from kitchens to linen cupboards, visiting rooms to see that they were properly cleaned and in order. Beneath her there existed a whole staff of officers—Monsieur Beck, Olivier, Alphonse, Georges, Frank and Edouard who ran the restaurant and the grill, the bar and the kitchen. Some of them were nearly as old as herself, and all of them had been with her for many years because they felt as she felt about the Paris Ritz. It had always been and must continue to be the best, most luxurious hotel in the world, the model for all others.

And so, when the panic and exodus began, life inside the Ritz remained unchanged. Madame Ritz, with her dogs and canaries, stayed behind, and at her side stayed Monsieur Beck, Olivier, Alphonse and Georges, Frank and Edouard. Nothing short of the end of the world could have disturbed them. In a way, although they had a loyalty to France because only in France could they have conceived and carried out this work of art, the Ritz, they had no nationality. Alsatian, Austrian, Swiss, French, Italian in origin, they belonged to a world of no nationality or rather of all nationalities, perhaps the only true international world that existed—a world, in a sense, above national feelings or jealousies or bitterness.

In the bar most of the old faces turned up to play backgammon and drink and plot and intrigue—the gigolos, the White Russians, the superannuated kept women, a few men in uniform. In the great Baroque dining-room on the Place Vendôme side the same old faces appeared, the South Americans, the weary, bewildered French *noblesse*, and a few rich refugees still not believing in the fall of Paris. The band, depleted by two men who were somewhere in a defeated retreating army, played Viennese waltzes and the music from *Les Trois Valses* and out of nostalgic *Phi-Phi*. A waiter or a chambermaid here and there had disappeared, but the unbelieving, unbelievable world of the Ritz continued to survive. One saw Madame Ritz, recognized or unrecognized, with her Pekinese trotting beside her, in the long corridor bordered by show-cases with jewels and furs, or at the entrance to the grill or the great dining-room, seeing that everything went calmly and well, as if the world were not coming to an end. The sight of her reassured people, gave them the feeling that things could not be as bad as they seemed.

Outside, the streets were filled with people fleeing, carrying with them sewing machines and babies, mattresses and bedding, whatever they had managed in their panic to snatch up.

In the big *salon* of a suite facing the Place Vendôme, Anna put down the telephone and turned to Miss Godwin.

"It's odd," she said, "nobody answers at Lisette's house or at the Prefecture. There should be someone at the Prefecture."

Miss Godwin turned away from the window. "You can't

expect things to be running perfectly at a time like this." She turned back to the window again. "The crowd is worse than ever."

"Do you think they know something we don't know?"

"It's not likely. They haven't the friends you have. It's probably panic."

Anna got up and looked at herself in the mirror. It was no more than a worried gesture. She wasn't interested in her own face just now. She thought, "God damn it, I wish I knew what to do!"

Suddenly Miss Godwin was of no use to her. She could tell you who were the right people and how to behave and how to spend your money, but she did not know what to do when a war came along and things began to go to pieces. But then who did? Even the government didn't seem to know what to do or where it was going.

She turned again to Miss Godwin. "I suppose we ought to make up our minds what we are going to do—whether we're going to go or stay. Why don't you go and talk to Madame Ritz? Ask her."

Miss Godwin came away from the window and stood re-arranging the flowers in a big vase. "She didn't know anything at eleven—any more than we know."

"I'd try it anyway. I'd go myself but she's *your* friend. You've known her much longer than I have."

"Perhaps you're right. She may know something." Miss Godwin went out, closing the door behind her.

Anna didn't really want to know what was going on. She only wanted to be alone for a little while. She'd played a solitary game for so long that at moments like this she couldn't think or act properly unless she had a little time alone.

For the first time since Miss Godwin had come to her, she wished that she wasn't here, because after all Miss Godwin was old. You couldn't ask her to endure things you could endure. Anyway, she had been brought up differently. She couldn't take things the way Anna could. And now anything might happen —anything at all.

She wasn't frightened or alarmed. Indeed she had never in her whole life been frightened of violence, but only of people hurting her. The panic had never touched her. After all, the world couldn't go to pieces over night. If you had plenty of money you could buy your way out when and if the Germans came. But the worst thing was the boredom. For two days her very spirit had been corroded by it. She was aware only of an immense impatience for something, anything, to happen.

She walked up and down the big room, never troubling to look out of the big windows at the crowds pushing through the square. All these people had nothing to do with her. Their lives were apart, very remote now. They had nothing to do with her world, the world of the Ritz. But she was sick of that world too, which went round and round like a merry-go-round, always in frantic motion, always arriving at the same place.

She was bored, bored, bored, with the kind of boredom that was like a physical pain to which the pacing up and down alone brought relief.

And now to be trapped here with a telephone which did not function, with half her friends dispersed. She was filled with a sense of tremendous physical energy for which there was no outlet whatever. She thought, " What am I to do now ? Where am I to go ? What is to happen ? " She had a curious sense of being trapped at the end of a long narrow corridor in which someone—perhaps called Hitler—had shut and bolted a door against her.

She knew now that the feeling of boredom and of being trapped had been coming over her for a long time. That was the reason why for the past year she had been taking things to make her sleep. She thought, " I have everything I wanted, yet it is nothing at all."

Up and down, up and down the long room she walked in her wild restlessness. In her depression, everything seemed suddenly futile and dull—incredibly, sickeningly dull, worse even than the four years of sitting at home night after night with Ezra in Detroit until at last, sooner than she had expected, he was mercifully dead.

She tried the telephone again, thinking that this time she might have better luck and find someone to dine with her. But this time there was no service at all. The voice of the operator said, " I'm sorry, Madame. All private service has been suspended."

She put down the telephone and sat staring at it, the feeling of sickness sweeping over her once more. For one wild moment she thought, " I will go back home. Home to America." But quickly she dismissed the idea. She knew scarcely anyone there.

She would have to begin all over again and Miss Godwin was getting too old to be of much use. There wasn't anywhere to go in America, no home, no roots. She couldn't go back to Detroit, and certainly she couldn't go back all the way to Lewisburg, which represented all the roots she ever had.

Suddenly she began to cry, the tears pouring silently down her cheeks. It was unfortunate that she had thought of Lewisburg. She tried to stop crying but the tears still came. It was extraordinary, because she could not remember having wept since Tom and the baby died, years before.

She bent forward, her head cushioned in her arm, sobbing. She no longer heard the noise of the crowd with push-carts and bicycles and perambulators pouring through the square outside the window. She was frightened, by what she did not quite know unless it was the awful sense of her own loneliness and frustration and despair.

In the little *salon* under the mansard surrounded by the canaries in cages, Miss Godwin was having a good talk with Madame Ritz. Here on the garden side away from the street there were no sounds. The big trees came almost to the level of the little windows with the lace curtains and little pots of geraniums on the ledge. Up here, beneath the roof, one had no sense of being in Paris. The little room was more like a room in a house in Colmar or Mulhouse or Strasbourg, in the country from which Madame Ritz had come long ago as a young girl. Here, away from all the gilt and mirrors and crimson carpet, Madame Ritz was herself, the innkeeper's daughter from Alsace who knew how to run a fine inn and cared about nothing else in the world.

The friendship of the two women went back a long way, to the time when the Savoy was built in London and Miss Godwin's father was still alive and Miss Godwin had plenty of money. She was a young woman then, quite a little younger than Madame Ritz. Her father brought her to Europe after the death of her fiancé and they were the first guests to stay at the new hotel on the Thames. Monsieur and Madame Ritz had given a dinner for them on the night they arrived, because her father had known them well since the days of their first hotel in Italy.

While they talked, Madame Ritz, wearing horn-rimmed spectacles, kept working on a piece of *petit point*, concentrating all her attention upon it, yet hearing and answering everything

Miss Godwin said. The room was filled with earlier examples of her skill—a fire-screen, chair-backs and seats, worked in flowers in the eighteenth-century manner.

"I find it's good for nerves and concentration," she said. "When everything seems to be going to pieces, it has a way of pulling you together again. Getting exactly the right shade of wool in exactly the right spot becomes as important as the selection of the right cabinet minister.

"Sometimes," she added cynically, "it turns out to be *more* important. I've always thought that was one of the great qualities of the French—that in the very midst of confusion and revolution and disaster they go right on making beautiful clothes and painting pictures and turning out exquisite furniture. It gives you a sense of proportion and something to steer by. People are born and grow up and make trouble and kill each other off, but the effort you put into a chair or table or a piece of music goes on for ever. Immortality is what you leave behind in accomplishment, not just what becomes of you. The trouble is that most people are so small-minded and egotistical, they're always saying, 'What is to become of *me*? Is there a Heaven waiting for *me*? Is it possible that *I* can die?' All that is nonsense and of no importance. It would be much better if they settled down to *doing* something, *making* something that would last long after they're dead."

Listening to this sudden outburst of philosophy, Miss Godwin thought, "There is something she's not telling me . . . something she doesn't want to talk about. She's trying not to talk about it. But that something is what I have to know."

So she said, "Mrs. Bolton is very upset . . . not afraid or panicky . . . but sick and bored and bewildered. She doesn't know what she should do. It's not easy to know. She can be very difficult. There are all her furs and jewels—they're worth an enormous amount of money. I don't think that worries her as much as it worries me."

There was a little silence and Madame Ritz without looking up said, "I've never known anything of Mrs. Bolton's background. I don't know what to advise you. Things like background make a great difference. I only know she is a very rich, good-looking woman who seems only interested in amusing herself. There is something I would like to ask. You need not answer me unless you like."

" Yes ? " said Miss Godwin.

" Is Mrs. Bolton of the people or is she simply a rich, spoiled woman who knows nothing and knows how to do nothing ? "

" She is of the people," said Miss Godwin. " Her father was a *petit fonctionnaire*, her mother a *femme de ménage*. Her money came through a second marriage. You are the first person I have ever told that. She does not even know that I know it."

The information was interesting enough to make Madame Ritz put down her *petit point*, push the spectacles up on her forehead and say, " *Tiens !* Over here she would have been a dressmaker or a kept woman. I suppose in America with divorce so easy, men marry women instead of keeping them."

" I'd never thought of it like that. Does it make a difference in what you'd advise . . . I mean what I told you just now ? "

Madame Ritz did not take up her work again. She said, " Yes. I'd advise you to call the motor, put into it everything you can and go to England or America. I can take charge of the trunks that are left. Of course, I can't swear what will happen to them in the long run."

Miss Godwin was aware again that her friend knew something she was not telling her.

" You believe me, don't you," asked Madame Ritz, " that that is the best course ? "

" Yes," said Miss Godwin doubtfully.

" But you don't," said Madame Ritz. As if to make what she was saying impressive, she put aside the *petit point* altogether and placed the spectacles on a table beside her.

" Listen to me," she said, " *Ecoutez-moi bien*, Miss Godwin. This isn't like the last war. This is going to be like the end of Europe. When it's over the old life will be gone for ever. The last war destroyed a lot of things but this time there won't be anything left but fragments. You . . . you and your Mrs. Bolton won't want to see what is left. You won't want to see it ever again. It will be ugly, with no place for people like you. It isn't like the last war. Then there were remnants of decency left in Germany. It was bad enough because Germans are always Germans, but this time they are monsters. They will do things . . . even a few of the French politicians will do things that are not to be believed . . . because for all of them this war is their last chance . . . their very last."

She stood up and went to the window. " A cousin of mine

turned up yesterday. He had escaped from the trap around
Abbeville. He sat here for two hours telling me what it was
like. I have lived through all kinds of things but I have never
heard anything like it. I have told no one of this but you. It
wouldn't do any good. It would only make more panic. If I
were you and Mrs. Bolton, I would get out quickly—now—
each day it will be worse. Anything at all can happen. There is
no reason to stay. It has nothing to do with either you or
Mrs. Bolton. You will only be in the way."

" And you ? " asked Miss Godwin.

Madame Ritz shrugged her shoulders. "For me it does not
matter. I won't live to see the end of it in any case. This is
my hotel. My husband and I made it. It is our immortality.
Three hundred years from now the name Ritz will still be a
name meaning what it means everywhere in the world. You
see, I couldn't leave the hotel. Without it I would have nothing
and be nothing. I would cease to exist. To go away would
be like suicide." After a moment she said, "After all, I am
French."

Suddenly Miss Godwin understood why Madame Ritz was
looking out of the window. The old woman was crying.
But she managed to control herself and say, "I've seen the
people who have been running things in this world for more
than fifty years. I've known most of them, some of them very
well indeed. Most of them were *voyous*, no-goods, but wielding
a lot of power. Now they've brought the world crashing down
on their own heads by their own selfishness, their own triviality
—their greed, their folly. It's all over. Once it was a nice
pleasant world—for a few people. I should be grateful to them,
for they made my fortune, mine and my husband's, but I am
not. I hate them bitterly." She turned towards Miss Godwin.
"No, take your Mrs. Bolton and all the people like her and
get out while you can. It is going to be ugly. Before it is
finished bodies will be hanging from lamp-posts outside there
in the Place Vendôme—in front of the entrance to the Ritz and
the Morgan Bank. It's all over."

She crossed the room and took Miss Godwin's hand. "Now
go ! I'll say good-bye now. You'll be busy. Get out as
soon as you can."

Then the two women embraced each other. They had
never been on terms as intimate as that, but they had been

speaking to each other in a new way, as two civilized people who understood what few of the others in the panic-stricken city understood. That had brought them very close together.

Madame Ritz went to the door with Miss Godwin and stood there looking after her until she disappeared. Then she called the two Pekinese who had strayed down the hall, pushed them gently into the room, closed the door and returned to her work.

When Miss Godwin opened the door of the *salon* in the Place Vendôme suite, she saw that Anna had been crying. She had never before seen Anna weep and the sight warmed her heart, not because she took any pleasure in the sight of her companion's fear or unhappiness but because it made her seem human. Tactfully she ignored the signs and reported what Madame Ritz had said.

When she had finished Anna said, " All right. Let's get out then. We might as well do that as anything else. At any rate it will be better than sitting here doing nothing, listening to rumours. I don't give a damn what happens. I only wish to God something would—anything at all ! "

Before she could change her mind, Miss Godwin took up the telephone and called the room of the driver. He was an elderly Auvergnat called Georges Legraval. He was waiting in his room for some decision. He himself wanted to get out. He wanted action ; action of any kind was better than waiting . . . waiting . . . waiting while Paris disintegrated.

His voice was almost eager, " I can get the car and be back in half an hour."

Miss Godwin put down the telephone and turned to Anna. " He will be here in half an hour. We should be able to make Blois before dark."

Then she went about the business of collecting the luggage and getting their papers together. She was both experienced and orderly. They had the proper visas for any frontier whatever. While she worked the sound of the refugees outside the windows seemed to increase ; it was as if the sound spread all over Paris, over all the world—a kind of remote, gigantic humming, punctuated by the occasional sharp protest of an automobile horn.

Anna collected her books, her jewel case, a small overnight bag. Once she said, " God damn this war ! God damn everything ! "

[68]

"Have you thought where we shall head for?" asked Miss Godwin.

"No. What difference does it make?"

"Only we have to think of where we can sail from if the thing spreads. There is Spain and there is Marseilles."

"It won't be that bad," said Anna. "It'll be over in a little while. They'll be able to hold somewhere."

Miss Godwin ignored her. "If it's Spain, we should head for Biarritz. If it's Marseilles, Monte Carlo or Cannes would be the place."

Her voice was a little sharp with impatience. She was aware suddenly that Anna was not only annoyed but frightened, not by the prospect of flight and immediate, concrete dangers but by something else. She was not behaving well; she was jittery and selfish and irritable. The sound of her voice was sharp and edgy against the low confused humming sound from the city outside the window. As she worked Miss Godwin thought, "She is afraid because there is no place to go. The only world in which she had ever made a place for herself is falling apart." There *was* no other world—nothing to go back to.

Miss Godwin's thoughts ran on, "Most people have a place to turn to. Usually they go back to their own roots. But she can't. There is no place to go." And suddenly it became clear to her, how deformed was Anna's whole existence, how perverted, how distorted it was, how tragic a waste of energy, of intelligence, of health, of force she represented.

In a little while they telephoned from below-stairs to say that the driver, Legraval, was there with the car. The porter came for the few bags they were taking with them. Miss Godwin checked the arrangements for storing the trunks with the concierge.

As they walked through the main corridor the sound of music came out of the main dining-room. The orchestra was playing a potpourri of Offenbach, the tinkling, gas-lighted music of the Second Empire which had been so like this world crashing about them. The place was nearly empty. A few old women in wigs or dyed hair sat at the tables having tea.

Miss Godwin thought, "Old witches sitting about, like hags at a wake."

[69]

The driver kept as much as possible to the back streets all the way across Paris to the Porte d'Orléans. It wasn't only that the main streets were uncomfortably crowded with refugees but that many of the refugees were unpleasant, and turned menacing at the sight of the big black Rolls-Royce occupied by a driver and two women. A Paris mob, Miss Godwin knew, could be the nastiest mob on earth. It could be fickle and vicious and violent and unreasoning.

Even after they passed the Porte d'Orléans it was possible to stick to back streets through the suburbs, taking the long way round but making better progress. Only when they were twenty miles south of the city was it necessary to return to the main road south.

From then on the progress of the flight was uncertain. At times the road would be clear for a little way or only encumbered by a few stray, slow-moving cars or push-carts, or a knot of neighbours, or families fleeing south. Then suddenly it would be cluttered and jammed and the car would be forced to crawl at a snail's pace or stop altogether.

Each time this happened strange faces crowded about the windows and peered in, making rude or threatening remarks. These were violent people, angry not only at their betrayal and because they were bewildered and terrified, but angry and resentful of everything the big car represented. Once a child threw a handful of pebbles against the windows and once an old woman with a witch-like face, framed in straggly hair, spat against the glass. The spittle hung there and dried at last in the heat and dust.

Only the two American flags flying from the fenders prevented them from worse things. The driver, a tough old man, explained fiercely and falsely that the ladies in the car were from the American Embassy, ordered to leave Paris by the government.

Again and again the word " *gouvernement* " brought cries of mockery and abuse. " *Le gouvernement ! Les salauds ! Ces voyous !* " and worse things.

In the back of the car Anna and Miss Godwin did not talk much. They were both tired with a weariness that was curious and indescribable but closely related to despair.

Anna, watching the people along the roadside, staring back at the shrewd faces which peered in at the window of the car, felt no fear but only a kind of confusion and bewilderment. She thought, " I do not belong here on the inside. I am one of *them*. I belong with them pushing a baby carriage or a cart."

She looked down at her hands, beautiful with the lacquered nails and the huge and famous emerald. Now she regarded them with a curious sense of revulsion, as if they were not her hands at all but strange ones which had somehow been grafted upon the stumps of her arms. And suddenly as she looked at them they turned into her mother's hands, dried and red and cracked by cleaning fluid, hands which she knew as well as her own and which, despite their roughness and callousness, had a kind of beauty. An artist, a real painter would have preferred them to these white long-nailed fingers which were her own.

A thousand times during the past five years, when she had sat at the head of a table surrounded by notorious, fashionable people, people whose names were in the news, she had thought, " If Momma could only see me now, she'd be proud. She'd see that I became *somebody* in the world. She'd see that I had got what she wanted me to have in life."

But now suddenly it was different. She knew that her mother wouldn't be proud of her right now. She knew for the first time that this woman riding in a rich car, wearing expensive clothes and jewels, was not at all what her mother, Mary Scanlon, the charwoman, had wanted her to be. No, it was not this that the warm, honest Mary Scanlon had pictured while she scrubbed floors and washed curtains so that her daughter Annie could go to school. Mary Scanlon had never wanted to " show Lewisburg." She had wanted her daughter to be successful, honourable, rich—yes, but by her own efforts, not by the accident of marrying a rich old man.

No, Anna knew she belonged outside of the glass, walking along the dusty highway with the people. Now, fleeing Paris, she was alone . . . utterly, absolutely alone. She had no roots ; she belonged nowhere. It was all over. The curtain was coming down on the last act, with the stage in ruin and disorder, the cast dispersed. That was the only thing that frightened her— not the fleeing mob, nor the Germans, nor even the menacing faces at the windows of the car.

That is exactly the way she described it to me. " All the way until the Germans machine-gunned us, I sat there in the car hating myself. I don't think you can understand what that is like—to loathe yourself, utterly and completely."

The sun went down behind the poplars lining the road and the long slow twilight of Northern France began—that slow twilight which is like the soft descent of an azure-coloured mist. The farther the car travelled from Paris, the greater became the crowds and confusion along the roads. Here and there, pushed aside into the ditch by the roadside, were abandoned cars and delivery vans, out of petrol or with shattered tires. Among the refugees there now appeared soldiers still carrying their rifles, trudging along on foot without formation.

Legraval, who talked to one of them, said they had lost their regiment but were bound south to the Loire in the hope of making a stand there.

The horror came just as the twilight deepened into the borders of darkness. It was heralded by the first distant sound of aeroplane motors high up in the darkening sky. Inside the car, Anna and Miss Godwin could not hear the sound. They discovered only that the people outside—the old men and women, the children, the soldiers, were all looking upward towards something. Anna leaned forward to ask Legraval what it was.

"Aeroplanes," he answered. "They're probably our own. It's too dark to identify them." He leaned forward and put out the lights of the car. "Just to make sure," he added.

Then suddenly the sound of the planes became audible inside the car, with a sickening rush and swoop of sound that mounted quickly into a roar and a shriek punctuated by the rattle of machine-gun fire.

"They're Boches," screamed Miss Godwin. "Get down on the floor." And she slipped to the floor pulling Anna with her. Outside a terrifying, indescribable noise arose all round the stalled car, a bedlam of screams and the sound of dogs howling, all mixed with the swooping scream of the planes and the rattle of fire from machine-guns, punctuated at sharp intervals by the explosion of a small bomb.

Then suddenly it was all over and above the confusion of sound outside rose the single, sustained, high-pitched wail of an old woman.

In the half-darkness Anna said, " Are you all right ? "
" Yes."

" And you, Georges ? "

" Yes, Madame." And then his stoic Auvergnat growl, " Oh, *les cochons ! Les salauds !* Shooting children and old women. Oh, *les salauds ! "* And a flow of much more obscene language.

The car was standing still now, in the midst of the confusion and noise. The long, high-pitched wail of the old woman still continued.

Anna leaned forward. " We'd better see if we can help, Georges." She opened the door and stepped out. In the dim light she saw in the ditch an old man lying flat out, his arms outstretched, on the bank alongside the road. She knew he was old by the whiteness of his beard and hair. She knew by the way he lay that he was dead. Then she saw that the top of his head was blown away.

A little way from him, three or four people huddled over a woman and a child. All along the ditch there were dimly outlined huddles of people. The old woman who was wailing sat on the edge of the ditch beside the dead old man, her grey face uplifted towards the sky. Near by a wounded fox terrier bitch howled and kept going round in circles trying to bite her side.

Then suddenly it was too dark to see any longer and there was only the wild confused sound of shrieks and moaning and Legraval was beside her with a torch.

" There's a child hurt over there," said Anna. On her high heels she stumbled over along the uneven edge of the road to the little group. Legraval followed her and turned the torch on the little huddle of people gathered about a child and a middle-aged woman. The woman was already quite dead, her body cut almost in half by machine-gun bullets, but the child, a girl of seven or eight, was alive, terrified and crying, with the blood pouring from her skull.

" Here, give me the light," said Anna to the driver. " Pick her up and carry her to the car." Then she kicked off the shoes that troubled her.

" There's a woman over there," said a voice out of the darkness, and Anna with the torch found a woman lying unconscious on the bloodstained bank of the road. In the circle of light from the electric torch, the red blood glistened on the summer grass.

Near by the old woman still wailed. The fox terrier had ceased howling and trying to bite her side. She was dead. Bending over the woman was an old man.

Anna said to the man, " Help me get her to my car. I'll take her feet." And to Miss Godwin, who had followed her, " Take the torch."

Together, Anna holding the woman's dusty feet clad in black woollen stockings and worn dusty shoes, and the old man her shoulders, they got her on to the seat.

Already a woman with a small girl was in the seat beside Legraval's place. Anna put the woman's feet on the ground and helped the old man to drag and carry her into the car. She was very strong, stronger than the old man. Together they managed to get the woman into the car and then on to the seat.

A crowd had gathered round the car, among them some who had been wounded. It was a big car, there would be plenty of room. Already in the front there were three in the seat beside Legraval. Others attempted to crowd into the back. Legraval kept yelling at them but in the confusion and panic they paid no attention. And then suddenly a big man forced the others aside, largely by the sound of his voice. He kept shouting, " Make way ! Out of the way ! " He was carrying a woman whose head fell back across his strong arms. Her arms and legs dangled helplessly. The man's shirt had been torn half off him and the white skin of the powerful arms and chest showed pale in the darkness. Close behind him there was an ugly little man in the blue uniform of the French Army. He was carrying a baby.

Legraval was getting nowhere with his shouting. It only added to the uproar without achieving anything.

Anna, placing herself before the car door, cried out, " Wait ! The car is full ! "

But the man's deep voice answered her quietly, " There is room for her ! There has to be room for her ! "

Then Anna turned the electric torch on his face. She opened her mouth to speak but no words came out. She felt suddenly faint and leaned against the car, letting the torch fall to the ground at her side. For what she had seen was Tom Harrigan—a big man with blue eyes and dark, curly hair, carrying a woman who Anna knew at once was already dead.

He pushed past her and laid the woman on the floor of the car. Then he closed the door and said to the driver, " Turn round ! We're going back to Villiers."

Anna protested, "We're headed for Blois. It's dangerous to go back."

But the man only said, "To Villiers! Turn round!"

"This is my car," said Anna fiercely. "We are going ahead."

In the dusk he looked at her. She could not see his eyes but she knew that his face was very near to hers and that he was staring at her.

He said, in a very quiet voice, "You're going where I tell you. I know your kind. You're the cause of everything." And suddenly he slapped her hard on the side of the face.

Miss Godwin screamed and the old driver called out nervously, "We'd better go back. It's nearer. Get on the running board, Madame, and hang on to the side." It was impossible for old Georges to consider defending his mistress against this big man.

For a moment Anna stood quite still, holding her hand to her face. The blow had a curious effect upon her. At first she wanted to strike back, to scratch and kick him as she had learned so well to do in her childhood in the river flats. Then suddenly she thought, "He is right. I do not matter at all. It doesn't matter which way I go or really what happens to me. I am of no importance." The wonderful thing was that something had happened, something with a sense of reality.

With her hand still against her face she said to the driver, "All right, we'll go back to Villiers." The man clung to the running board a little behind Miss Godwin.

At the crossroads a hundred feet ahead the big car managed to turn round. The uproar along the road still continued. The crowd kept getting in the way, but at last the car managed to get free and to move slowly back through the confusion towards the town of Villiers.

Side by side on the running board, Anna and Miss Godwin clung to the doors of the car. Neither of them spoke but kept peering ahead as the car without lights now moved slowly along the road with its horn adding to the din.

Villiers was a small town. It had no hospital and so Legraval went with the political instinct of a Frenchman to the Mairie—a little, ugly building of stucco and brick on the high road. It was only two miles from the spot where the slaughter had occurred, but the journey seemed interminable.

For Anna, the whole thing, the screams, the dead old man, the screeching old woman, the cries and the crowd, had no reality. She kept seeing the big man, illumined for the fraction of a minute by the electric torch. There was no longer any pain in her own face. She felt no anger but only a kind of vague happiness and excitement and satisfaction, as if for years she had been awaiting violence and blood and death. She was aware that her hands, those beautiful hands, were sticky and that the stickiness was blood.

Inside the car one of the women kept moaning and crying out, but the woman on the floor made no sound.

At the Mairie, there were already two other cars, a butcher's truck and a little Citroen, both laden with wounded. The Mayor appeared, a plump, muddled, ineffective little old man, and an elderly doctor, too old for military service. People shouted and screamed. The crowd kept increasing in size, from along the road and out of the houses of the village.

The car stopped in the Mairie courtyard and suddenly the big man appeared again. At sight of him Anna said, " Tell me what to do ? " She felt him looking at her again in the darkness and then he said in a gentle voice, " Help me to get my wife inside." He spoke French with a very faint accent.

She forgot about Miss Godwin. She forgot everything but the dead woman and what the man asked of her. It was as if she were hypnotized by the memory of his face in the circle of light from the electric torch. She kept thinking, " It couldn't be. He couldn't look that much like Tom. It's something I imagined."

Miss Godwin was neither lost nor hysterical. Somehow she had discovered the wife of the Mayor and set about organizing the situation and collecting disinfectant and sheets for bandages.

It was not easy. The women who remained in the village were small people to whom their linen was a precious thing. A few gave stuff freely but most of them were hesitant and with them Miss Godwin knew the answer. Inside her blouse she had pinned all the money for their flight—banknote after banknote of big denomination. With any one of these a woman could replace the linen for a whole household. In a little while virtually all the supplies of the village were at the Mairie. It was as if Miss Godwin too had been waiting for this occasion to display her efficiency and talent for organization.

Inside there were lights, for the windows had been covered

long ago against just such an occasion. The wounded were laid out on the floor of the Mayor's office and the big room adjoining it.

In the Mayor's office, the big man laid the woman he had been carrying tenderly on the floor, placing a law book behind her head.

But she was already dead. Anna saw now that there was no doubt. She must have been killed by the first bullet that struck her. She was a young woman, not more than twenty-five or thirty, rather cheaply but smartly dressed and very pretty, with blonde hair done simply in a braid around her head. The man took up one of the small limp hands and pressed it between his. He felt the wrist and looked down at the woman's face and then very gently folded the hands across the woman's breast, and buried his head in his arms and sobbed.

At the sight Anna turned away. At first when they came into the lighted room, it seemed to her again for a second that he looked like Tom, as Tom might have looked if he had lived. When she looked at him again he was kneeling beside the dead woman with his back to Anna. The dark head and the back of the neck and the broad shoulders were very familiar. They had the same look of strength and assurance she remembered. But the face was quite different—a strong, rather lean face, dark with large burning blue eyes. She thought, "He is not French." But she could not guess the nationality.

There was nothing to do. She stood there feeling useless and foolish, aware that somewhere she had lost her hat and her handbag and shoes, that her clothes were soiled with blood and dust and that the blood was still on her hands. Her feet were cut and bruised by the gravel of the courtyard before the Mairie.

From nowhere the ugly little man in the sergeant's uniform, carrying the baby, had appeared. He was standing there now, a thin scraggly dark little fellow. The baby was awake but not crying. It could not have been more than two or three months old. The little man looked at Anna and then said quietly in a low voice, " She was his wife. He loved her very much."

Then instinctively, without knowing why she did it, Anna laid one hand on the shoulder of the man who looked like Tom and said, " I will take care of the baby." She did not know why she said it. It was as if she heard someone else speaking.

At first he did not appear to notice or even to hear her, but

[77]

after a little while he stopped sobbing and stood up. For a moment he said nothing but stood looking at her in the same direct honest way Tom had had long ago—the look of a simple honest man who had nothing to be ashamed of. It was as if, still a little dazed, he was trying to discover how she had come there, what she was, as if he were attempting to penetrate the very essence of her being.

Then he said quietly, " I am very sorry I struck you. I apologize. I thought I could save my wife's life. It was all for nothing. Please, will you forgive me ? "

Anna said, " Don't think of that. It was nothing."

He looked at her again. " You said you would care for the baby ? "

" Yes."

" That would be a great help just now. A man doesn't know much about babies. Where are you going from here ? "

Then a strange thing happened to Anna. She heard herself saying, " I am going back to Paris."

" I thought you were running away."

" I was, but I am going back now."

He still stared at her out of the eyes which were so much like Tom's. " What are you, English ? " he asked.

" No. American."

" That is better. It will be easier for you."

Then Anna heard herself speaking again, saying words which in a way had not come into her head at all. She was saying, " I can take the baby with me and care for it until you make other arrangements. Has it any grandparents ? "

" No," said the man in a dull voice, " there is no one."

Out of long habit, half-consciously, she was trying to discover what world he came from, where he belonged. She was searching for a label, one of those labels which everyone had in her world ; but there was none. He stood there in the dim light in army trousers and torn shirt, no cap on the tousled dark hair, tall and rather handsome, his big shoulders drooping a little. It was impossible from the uniform trousers to know even whether he was an officer or not. He was simply a man who looked and acted and spoke like Tom.

" I could pay you for his keep," he said.

" No. That wouldn't be necessary."

How could she explain to him that what he could pay her

would mean nothing at all, that what he paid her for a month would be less than she would spend in a day at the hairdresser's?

He said, " You see, I am on my way to the Loire. I am an engineer. I have been sent to blow up the bridges."

" It's as bad as that? "

" It's as bad as that." And then after a moment, " Do you still mean to go back to Paris? "

" Yes."

He looked down again at the dead woman, almost as if he were attempting some communication with her. Then as if overcome he turned away and went out of the room without saying anything. The little man still held the baby who began to cry dully, quietly, as if from weariness.

Anna took the child from the little man and said, " Perhaps he's hungry. Is there anything to feed him? "

" I don't know," said the little man. " I don't know anything about babies. There was some tinned milk. I don't know what became of it."

The feel of the child in her arms produced an extraordinary effect upon Anna. She began to rock it gently and it stopped crying to look up at her gravely out of its blue eyes.

" Perhaps I can find milk in the village. Will he come back, do you think . . . the father, I mean? "

" Yes."

" Where did they come from? " asked Anna.

" Lambert is his name . . ." said the little man. " Captain Jean Lambert . . . he belongs to a regiment of sapeurs. I am his orderly. When everything went to pieces up north we were ordered south to the Loire, to get there however we could. When he knew how bad things were, we made our way to Paris and he picked up his wife and the baby there. We started out in his car but it broke down just the other side of here. We couldn't repair it so we set out on foot. He wouldn't leave them. He loved his wife very much."

Slowly order came out of the confusion in the Mairie. Miss Godwin was a tower of strength, organizing things, tearing sheets into bandages, washing wounds. The old doctor did his fumbling, palsied best. Out of nowhere appeared two Sisters of St. Joseph, one an old woman and the other a young nun with a pale, almost transparent face.

Six of the wounded died within an hour or two. Some of the others would survive if care could be given them soon.

It was the young nun, Sister Angelique, who went with Anna to find dried milk for the baby. They found it at the village *épicerie* where the fat proprietress provided a bottle and nipple and hot water from the *pharmacie* next door. Anna carried the baby with her and herself fed it and changed it and put it back to sleep again. The milk appeared to agree with it for it slept soundly in Anna's arms until she put it on the bed of the proprietress of the *épicerie*. Then she returned to the Mairie to find the Captain. It was daylight when she discovered him, wandering up and down beneath the pollarded linden trees of the Mairie courtyard.

She had washed her hands and face and redone her hair and rid her clothes of as much dust and blood as possible. From the woman who kept the *épicerie* she bought a pair of worn shoes much too big for her. When the man saw her he started to turn away and then as he recognized her, he turned back. He wore an old black coat which he had found somewhere and put on over his torn shirt. But even in the tattered dirty clothing there was a kind of magnificence about him—the same physical glow and splendour that Tom had always had. She saw suddenly that in this more than in anything else the likeness lay. He had, it was true, the same blue eyes and dark curly hair and slightly pointed ears, but it was something in the carriage, in the way he looked at you.

For a moment he stared at her and as she waited she thought, "I will never see sorrow like this again." And back across the years came rushing that terrible sensation of black misery which she had felt at the news of Tom's death. She experienced a wild desire to ease the pain, to help him in some way. But there was nothing she could do. In such sorrow one was, she knew well enough, for ever alone.

She said, "The baby is asleep. I gave him a bottle. He seems all right."

"Where is he now?" he asked.

"At the *épicerie*."

"I'll say good-bye to him and then be on my way."

She looked at him in surprise and, understanding her glance, he said, "It's all over now. It's all taken care of. The priest and the nuns have arranged for it. There is nothing I can do.

[80]

I should be already at the Loire." Then after a moment he said, " They have taken her to the house of the Mayor. I have said good-bye to her."

They walked in silence to the *épicerie* and there in the proprietress's bedroom at the back of the shop they stood together over the bed where the baby lay sleeping.

The man stood for a time looking down at him and then said, " *Au revoir, petit !* " in a low voice.

Anna said, " You do not know my name."

" No. It would be good of you to give it to me."

So they borrowed a pencil and a bit of brown paper from the proprietress, and she wrote it down :

Mrs. EZRA BOLTON
The Hotel Ritz
Paris.

As he took the paper she noticed his hands. They were big but beautiful. He read the name and the address and then looked at her very directly.

" Thank you," he said coldly, " I will take the baby off your hands as soon as possible."

She felt the colour rising in her cheeks and realized that she was ashamed because the Ritz Hotel was the only adddress that she had to give him. She felt suddenly shabby and cheap and aware sharply of the barrier that had arisen between them again. She heard him saying, " It is your kind that have caused all the trouble."

She wanted desperately to cry out, " I'm not like that really. My mother was a charwoman. I came from the people really." But that would only sound hysterical and silly.

" And if I wanted to find you ? " she asked.

" Of course," he said quickly ; " I'm sorry." And she had the feeling that he meant her to know that he was sorry too for his rudeness.

He wrote on a bit of paper :

JEAN PIERRE LAMBERT
Capitaine Onzième Sapeurs
103 Rue de Bolivie
Paris XV.

" That is where we lived," he said. " There will be no one there now but the concierge will probably know where I am."

Then he looked at her as if he felt there should be some explanation. "My wife," he said, "was an Austrian. She came to Paris with her father . . . they were refugees. He was an old man—a Social Democrat. He died a year ago. She hadn't any real friends in Paris."

Then again she thought, "But despite the name, he really isn't French at all," And she said, "Are you French?"

"No," he said, "I am French by naturalization. I am Russian by birth. My parents were refugees after the last war. I was a boy when I came to Paris."

Then standing there in the grey chill morning light under the linden trees there came to her for the first time a vague sense of destiny, a feeling that somehow she had at last found her place in the world. She knew suddenly what it was she had to do.

He went away and she stood watching him until he disappeared among the refugees who still streamed along the dusty poplar-bordered road away from Paris, and as he disappeared, she experienced a sudden feeling of sickness and loss. She had wanted passionately to help him and she had found no way, and now he was gone with the chances very good that she would never see him again. It was all unreasonable, perhaps even hysterical, but nothing like it had happened to her for a long time.

They first saw the German soldiers just outside the Porte d'Orléans, standing there in their clumsy grey-green uniforms, looking more alien against the grey of the old Paris houses than Bedouins or Hottentots would have looked. From the long abandoned *douane*, a soldier stepped and barred their way. When the car came to a stop, an officer appeared, lean, hard-faced and arrogant, rather astonished at the sight of a motor, a rich motor, coming *into* Paris.

Miss Godwin spoke to him in her excellent German. She explained that they were returning to Paris with a baby whose mother had been killed and five people who had been wounded in an attack made upon helpless refugees by German dive-bombers. She said this simply as a fact without recrimination but the flatness of the statement made it all the more forceful. The face of the officer turned faintly pink.

At first the officer was for turning them back, but the sight of so rich a car bedecked with tattered American flags, and the fact that the two women were Americans and obviously rich, roused in him the respect which lies in most Germans for whatever is big and rich and important. It may have been, too, that Miss Godwin's distinction and air of authority had something to do with it. With her uncompromising directness and rather dowdy clothes, she had the cold dignity and the assumption of power of a *hochgeborene Frau*. After a little bumptious show of authority he let them pass into the grey half-deserted city.

All the way to the Hotel Dieu neither Anna nor Miss Godwin, numbed by the shock of seeing German uniforms, said anything at all. The sight of a company of soldiers crossing the square before Notre Dame was something out of a nightmare. At the vast and dreary Hotel Dieu they left the five wounded passengers, a baker and his wife, a bus conductor, a small Jewish shopkeeper and a sewing woman. They were all effusive in their gratefulness. The baker tried to give Legraval twenty-five francs to help pay for the petrol.

It was tea time when they drove up before the door of the Ritz. There were no crowds of refugees now in the big square but only a boy on a bicycle and an old woman. Even here there was a grey-green sentry on duty. But he made no effort to stop them and, carrying the baby, Anna walked in ahead of Miss Godwin.

In the hall and main dining-room the orchestra was again playing the music of Offenbach. Here and there sat the old women in wigs or with dyed hair. It was exactly as if nothing had happened but for the German officers at tables among the wigs and dyed hair, having cocktails or tea. Those nearest to the entrance looked up and stared as Anna and Miss Godwin, untidy and dirty, came in the door.

The concierge greeted them with excitement. Alas, they could not have their own rooms. All the Vendôme side of the Ritz had been taken over by the German General Staff. Certainly there would be something for them on the Cambon side. He would call Madame Ritz.

In a moment, he put down the telephone saying Madame Ritz had asked them to come up to her.

She was waiting for them in the little room under the eaves and put down her embroidery and spectacles as they came in.

"So you came back?" she said quite directly, "And what have you been through? Where did you find the baby?"

In a rush of words Anna told the story.

"Put the baby on my bed," said Madame Ritz. She followed them into the bedroom and looked down at the baby, touching it gently with her fingertips as if it were something precious. "A fine baby! And very good. And now you must have something to drink. What do you wish—sherry or something stronger?"

"Scotch," said Anna and Miss Godwin surprisingly echoed her request.

"I should not have advised you to leave," said Madame Ritz. "In spite of what I told you I did not believe they would be so bad. I didn't believe they would come on so fast. They are worse even than in the last war."

She telephoned for the whisky and some sandwiches and then said, "I will see that you two get rooms on the Cambon side. There is someone there I should like to throw out. He has been entertaining German officers in the bar. Until I can get him out, you must stay here. You can have a bath and change your clothes. I will send for the luggage."

She was very calm, as if such things happened every day. She asked, "And what is the baby's name?"

Anna looked at Miss Godwin and then laughed, for the first time since they had left the Ritz. Then she said, "I don't know. In the excitement I forgot to ask. I have his father's name and address." She took out the bit of brown paper and handed it to Madame Ritz. The old lady put on her spectacles and looked at it, and then at Anna. "It is a somewhat disreputable quarter—*quelqu'onque*," she said, "certainly not distinguished. Perhaps you'll never hear from him again. Perhaps he's left a little gift on your doorstep."

Very quickly Anna said, "Oh, no! He's not like that. I shall see him again."

Madame Ritz gave her a quick, searching look and handed back the bit of paper. "Madame," she said, "you have more confidence in the human race than I have." Then the Pekinese began to bark wildly and turning to the door she said, "Come in!"

It was the waiter with the whisky.

Gerbevilliers was a little town, just off the main highway that ran southwards from Paris to Marseilles. In the old days, when the great rich cars raced back and forth from Nice and Monte Carlo and Cannes to Paris, the people of Gerbevilliers could see the white dust rising in clouds above the distant highway, but they lived far enough from it to remain always a sleepy, old town with one or two tiny factories, a convent, and a girls' boarding school. Above the town, on a small plateau, there was a brickyard, long since abandoned, and here, when the war began, the government sent the refugees without proper papers who had been driven out of Germany and Austria and Czecho-Slovakia.

It wasn't much of a place, what with the windows broken and brick dust everywhere, but after they had put up a fence of barbed wire, it was a convenient place to herd together all the homeless people who no longer belonged anywhere, whom nobody wanted, whom the politicians and especially the rich manufacturers did not want about because they were afraid of them. There were hundreds of thousands of them in France because France alone had received them as they streamed across the face of Europe, fleeing disaster and death.

In Gerbevilliers, at Number 123 Boulevard Victor Hugo, there was a small house with a dull nondescript façade. It had belonged to the notary, a worthy citizen called Monsieur André Picot, who had been away visiting his daughter in the north when the Germans swarmed over the border into Picardy. With his daughter he took to the road, but he got only as far as Beauvais when he was killed during the bombing.

The house was just a house, regarded as comfortable enough by the citizens of Gerbevilliers. It had a narrow passage running straight through it to the garden at the back, with a dining-room and kitchen on one side and a *salon* and bedroom on the other. Upstairs there were three bedrooms. The house had no bath-room and was heated by the kind of stove known as a *salamandre* which generates a furious heat for a yard or two. There was one of these in the dining-room and one in the *salon*. By leaving doors open a feeble heat penetrated the other rooms. The furniture was of the kind bought in suites at the Grand Bazaar de l'Hôtel de Ville, and the wallpaper was that peculiar combination of horrors designed for the French middle-class in which an immense and crawling vegetation spawned amid colours ranging from dun to dirty grey. The only redeeming feature was the garden and the view of the open country at the back, a view as French as any landscape by Claude Lorraine.

The little garden ran down to a clear deep little river where the brown trout hid in the writhing weeds. Beyond lay marshes and cress beds extending to a distant line of feathery poplars which bordered the Bois de Gerbevilliers.

It was a quiet landscape, peaceful and lost like the little town itself.

So there was excitement when a week after the fall of Paris a big black motor with two small American flags on the hood drove up, and out of it stepped an elderly driver, a distinguished grey-haired woman and a younger woman, smartly dressed, carrying a baby. The driver had a key to the notary's house. He opened the door and the three went inside. Thus Anna and Miss Godwin and the baby came to Gerbevilliers.

Within twenty-four hours the town knew all about them. It heard the details from Jeanne, the cleaning woman, from Marguerite, the cook, from the baker's wife, and the wife of the Mayor. They were Americans and both spoke excellent French. They were rich, which anyone could see from the car and driver. They had rented Monsieur Picot's house from his cousin, the *avocat*, who was vaguely a relation of the driver. They had come to Gerbevilliers to set up a canteen for the refugees who were struggling back from the south to their homes in the north, and for the wretched people in the concentration camp at the brickyard.

The rich car disappeared, since a rich car was no use if there was no *essence*, and two lorries appeared a few days later laden with all sorts of things—chocolate and cigarettes, medicines and even books. Part of them were unloaded at the Mairie and part of them at the house of the notary.

The Mayor, a gentle, bearded old man, an old-fashioned Socialist who wrote very bad and sentimental verse, had few observations to make concerning the newcomers. Remembering the activities of Americans during the preceding war he said, " The Americans are a strange people. They have plenty of money and they like giving away things." And he also said, " They must have very important friends in Paris, for Madame Bolton goes back and forth over the line between the zones with no trouble at all."

The line ran a little way to the north of Gerbevilliers. It divided France into two parts and was very difficult to cross. For crossing it without proper papers you could be imprisoned or even shot.

At the Mairie the refugees returning home were fed. There seemed to be an endless number of them, homeless, without money or shelter, virtually begging their way until the muddled government began a campaign of repatriation. At the Mairie they were fed with soup and bread, provided partly by the Mayor and the people of Gerbevilliers and partly by the government. The rest, the chocolate, the jams, the cigarettes, the medical supplies came from " *les Américaines* " who lived in the house of the notary.

The truth was that Anna had found something to do. She had great health and great energy and great ability as an executive, and now setting up a canteen gave her an outlet for all these qualities. She liked the trips to Lyons, to Orleans, to Paris, even as far as Marseilles and Geneva to buy soap and medicines, chocolate and cigarettes.

In those first weeks after the fall of Paris this was easy enough to do. She dealt in the beginning directly with manufacturers and wholesalers, dropping into offices where she bargained shrewdly. She bought heavily, for she was aware that before long the supply would give out and it would be difficult, even with influence, to get the things she needed. There were many discomforts, the misery of the crowded trains, and hotels, of sketchy meals and all-night trips. You couldn't any longer drive about the countryside in a big car, American flags or no American flags. But she scarcely noticed these things. In the sudden satisfaction of activity she felt alive once more ; there were even times when she almost found satisfaction in the complications and discomforts. And there was deep satisfaction, also, in coming to know people of all kinds whom she had never before encountered in France or anywhere in Europe.

During the first days in the notary's house she had planned vaguely to redecorate it. That was something she and Miss Godwin had always done with houses. During the long evenings when she sat with Miss Godwin in the ugly little *salon* while the baby slept in the next room, she planned how she would do away with the dreary crawling wallpapers, and replace the plain linen curtains with gay chintzes. Once she even went to the only shop in the town, but all the wallpaper and furniture there looked exactly like the stuff in the notary's house. She could not order things in Paris and have them sent on. There were too many difficulties about shipping things across the line between

[87]

the two zones. And the nearest big town with any sort of shops at all was Clermont and there was no time to go there.

Indeed there was no time for anything nowadays. When she was not away trying to buy up supplies, there was an endless amount of work to be done in the canteen at the Mairie, the visits to the awful brickyard where the foreign refugees were interned, the accounts to be kept, and a couple of hours a day to be given to the baby. Sometimes she and Miss Godwin even had refugees to stay a day or two in the extra bedrooms on the second floor— a pregnant woman who needed rest, or sick children, or an occasional old woman. Once they had an old woman who spent a week there before she was strong enough to be put aboard a train and shipped north. The old woman had come from a village near St. Quentin, fleeing nearly all the way on foot as far south as Périgueux.

" You would think," said Miss Godwin, " that the poor old thing had had enough of life. You'd think she'd want simply to lie down and die."

She had fled once before, twenty-five years earlier, half-way across France only to return and find her house in ashes and dust. Now she would return again to find the catastrophe repeated.

The odd thing was that she was very homesick. She talked of nothing but of going back to her village and her house. Anna, listening to her, had marvelled at the tenacity of her affection for the place in which she had been born and had lived all her eighty-three years. It was an emotion she herself had never experienced. Always, it seemed to her, she had wanted to escape from Lewisburg, from the awful house in Detroit, from one hotel and rented house after another.

During the fourth week of living in the notary's house they had a caller. He came in the late afternoon just after Anna had returned from one of her trips to Paris. Marguerite, the cook, looking very impressed, came in to announce him.

" It is the *Archiprêtre* of Moulins-la-Tarn," she said. " He asked if the American ladies would receive him. He is a very distinguished man—an *homme de lettres*. He has written many books on French history."

Anna was playing with the baby, and a little annoyed at being disturbed. She had no very happy memories of the church in Lewisburg nor any great fondness for priests. It had been years since she had heard Mass or gone to Confession. In the past ten years there had been times when she even concealed the fact that she had been born a Roman Catholic.

She hesitated for a moment but Miss Godwin said, " We shall have to see him. He represents the Church as the Mayor represents the State. That's important in this community."

Anna didn't protest. Long ago she had fallen into the habit of taking Miss Godwin's advice about such things. She said to Marguerite, " Tell him to come in ; and make some tea and bring in some cakes and sherry."

She did not know what she expected. Vaguely priests were always associated with the harsh, frustrated Irishman who had filled her childhood with the terror of purgatory and hell. In Lewisburg he had terrorized all the Poles and Italians and Irish of the Flats into giving large sums of money out of their scanty earnings. She thought, " Very likely he is coming for money."

But when the door opened, there appeared in the doorway a tall man of about sixty with fine blue eyes and white hair, whose charm flowed into the room like the warmth of a spring day.

Anna and Miss Godwin rose to greet him.

He said, quite simply, " I am Monseigneur Dubois, the *Archiprêtre* of Moulins-la-Tarn. I hope I am not being a nuisance by calling on you. I wanted to pay my respects to the two American ladies who are doing so much to help our unfortunate people."

They sat down again in the uncomfortable chairs, but something in the warmth of the *Archiprêtre's* appearance and personality made the stiff chairs of Anna and Miss Godwin seem comfortable, so comfortable that they were forgotten. There was no sense of nervousness about him, nor of any pomp or sanctity or piety. The French and Chinese have much in common in their civilized approach to the amenities of life. Both people have formulas with which to meet every situation —a meeting of strangers, a wedding, a birth, a death—formulas which are universal among their peoples and serve to carry one through any crisis with dignity and self-respect. The *Archiprêtre* now used the formula of weather, employed in meeting strangers.

He talked for a little time about the brilliance of the warm early autumn days and the curious blue light at dusk which was special to their part of the country. He remarked that fortunately it was a good year for crops, for France would need much food.

By that time Marguerite arrived with the tea and cakes and sherry and the last barrier of strangeness was down.

A little later Anna found herself telling him about the flight from Paris, the machine-gunning on the road, about Jean Lambert and the death of his wife, and finally of the baby.

" Miss Godwin and I found ourselves in Paris and suddenly neither of us wanted to escape. We wanted to do something useful. It was as simple as that. I really don't know quite how it happened but here we are."

" Gerbevilliers seemed a good place to come for a number of reasons."

Monseigneur Dubois did not say, " No doubt it was the hand of God," although Miss Godwin suspected that that was what he was thinking, quite sincerely. He used none of the clichés she expected from priests. He said, " Already you have done much for the poor people in the brickyard. The local people have tried to help but they are not rich, and sometimes they grow resentful over the high taxes. One can't blame them for that. They're already paying for the keep and the guarding of the poor people up there. At first, just after the catastrophe, some of them escaped and the townspeople hid them and passed them on to friends and relatives farther south, but that has been stopped now by the hand of the Boches and by the Vichy people. Your coming has been a great help. A cigarette, a piece of chocolate, it can make so much difference to the poor fellows up there." His face grew sad. " It makes them think they are not altogether forgotten."

He finished his glass of sherry and following again the formula of a first visit, which is never to stay more than half an hour, he said, " I must go now or I shall miss my bus. I do not know what Faith you are. That does not matter, but I should be glad to see you in church at Moulins. It is quite an interesting church—not beautiful but celebrated because of its antiquity and because it represents the transitional period between the Romanesque and Gothic in this part of France."

" I was born a Catholic," said Anna. " I am afraid I have not been too good a one for a long time."

The *Archiprêtre* smiled, " I should be glad to welcome you back." In the doorway he turned and said, " If you should like some books, I have quite a large library. I don't imagine the library of a notary amounts to much."

Anna smiled and said, " It amounts to nothing at all."

When he had gone the weariness had left both Anna and Miss Godwin. The visit left them with the impression that a very old friend whom they both loved had just left them. They had a new feeling about Gerbevilliers, that they had been accepted and belonged there.

Anna brought out the baby and gave him his supper and played with him until he fell asleep. Not knowing his name, they called him Jean Pierre after his father, from whom there was no news at all.

On the following Sunday she rose early, caught the bus, and heard Mass at Moulins-la-Tarn.

The autumn turned into winter slowly, in the French way, with a perceptible thickening of the chill afternoon fogs and a rim of white frost across the marshes. Black, heavy, crochetted shawls made their appearance on the plump round shoulders of Marguerite, the cook, and the thin ones of Jeanne, the charwoman, and the life of Gerbevilliers began to fall into a routine for Anna and Miss Godwin. Sometimes women from the town came to call and friendships sprang up—notably the friendship with the old Mayor who wrote bad verse, with Monseigneur Dubois, and with Madame St. Genis, wife of the baker.

She was a big, motherly woman, with greying hair and an enormous bosom, a kind of Ceres. She was a woman, too, of passionate feeling which she took little trouble to conceal. She hated the Germans and was for hanging the traitors to lamp-posts. Out of this period of Anna's life these three remained for ever fixed in her memory and her affections, I think because they were the first people who came into her existence at the period when she was, in a way, being born for the first time as a whole human creature. They were all a part of the life in Gerbevilliers which had begun really not in Gerbevilliers at all but at the moment when, in the midst of the human misery on the stricken road between Paris and Villiers, she had looked at her hands and thought suddenly, " These are not Annie Scanlon's hands at all. They belong to someone else who isn't and never was Annie Scanlon ! "

The hands weren't beautiful and white any longer, with shining and lacquered nails ; more often than not they were chapped and red with the chill of Gerbevilliers and the house of the notary. When she put cream on her hands and polish on the nails, Marguerite and Miss Godwin knew that it meant that she was going to Paris or to Vichy to see her powerful friends—the friends who made it easy for her to travel or to get money or to buy things which others could not buy.

They were not really friends and none knew this better than Anna herself. They were remnants of the old shattered life, people she had known, who had come to her dinners, with whom she had dined and spent week-ends, people off the *carrousel* which had begun going round and round long ago, back in 1918. It was astonishing how many of them there were, people with no loyalties and little honour, and how many of them had turned up in positions of power at the moment of betrayal and treason. Many of them were loathsome, but none knew better than Anna how useful they were. None knew better than she that without them it would be impossible to carry on with the only thing which any longer mattered to her. And she made a strange discovery—that she had never really belonged among them at all, that in reality she had always been an outsider, respected as she was respected now, only for her great wealth and perhaps a little for her beauty.

Once the knowledge might have roused fierce pride, but now that no longer seemed to matter. She had now to use them for something that was far more important to her than the spectacle which once had fascinated her.

Without giving any sign of noticing the change, Miss Godwin was aware of many things—that Anna was no longer nervous and irritable, that there were no longer moments when she said silly things, that she had become more beautiful, that for the first time there was a warmth in her. There were even moments when Anna revealed little fragments of the past—shattered, disconnected fragments about the strange dead life she had lived in Detroit as Ezra Bolton's wife, and even beyond that, about the time she had worked as a typist at twenty-five dollars a week. Beyond that she never went. There was never any mention of Tom or of Lewisburg. It was as if the scars had not yet healed completely.

And with the change in Anna the devotion of Miss Godwin increased; it was almost as if late in life she had discovered a daughter of her own. She became at times tiresome, urging

Anna not to go to the Mairie or the brickyard when the weather was bad. She took to making little delicacies herself over the ancient stove of the notary's little house, just for Anna. There grew up between the two women a curious new relationship in which they understood each other without speaking.

For Miss Godwin's character changed too. A little of the stiffness went out of her. She developed favourites among the refugees in the brickyard—one an old Jewish professor who was nearly blind, another a tubercular Austrian boy of twenty-three who had only a little while to live, a third a young violinist whose hands had been smashed by the Gestapo before he escaped.

Something had happened to Miss Godwin. It was as if for the first time she understood that there were in the world other people than those among whom she had spent her life—the people who lived in great houses and had daughters who must be "launched" in order to find rich husbands. Miss Godwin had always been a "lady" which perhaps Anna never quite succeeded in becoming, but she too had always been a little deficient in human warmth. Now when she set out through the drizzling rain to the Mairie or the brickyard, there was a kind of glow about her. The townspeople noticed her smiling to herself as she walked along the street.

She was thinking to herself how improbable her life had been, how extraordinary it was that at the very end of it there should have come this compensation, this excitement, this richness which she experienced each day when she wakened. There was first of all the baby, and then breakfast, and then the long trip up the hill to the brickyard to care for the old professor and the violinist and the boy dying of tuberculosis and all the others. There were times when it seemed to her that all the rest of her life had been wasted, that she had only begun to live now. A virgin of sixty-eight, she became suddenly mother to a whole world—the sad, decaying world of the brickyard, a world peopled by ghosts whom the rest of the world, even France which alone had given them refuge, had forgotten.

She was grateful now for Anna's money, even for the shallow, silly life Anna had led all those years, because the money and the people Anna had come to know during those years made all this possible. They had been a corrupt lot and those who remained in power in France were a corrupt lot, opportunists, all without loyalty. They were, after all, the only people Anna knew. Now it had turned out that they had a value. They could be used. She suspected that that was exactly what Anna was doing—using them.

That was why Anna went to Paris or to Vichy every week. That was why she stayed at the Ritz and got out her sables and jewels and went to dine at Maxim's with all the traitors, the collaborators and German officers. Somehow she was getting money when no other foreigner in Paris was allowed more than a pittance a week out of his own country. Somehow she was getting food for her refugees and the people in the concentration camp when food could not be bought even on the black market. Miss Godwin saw that suddenly Anna was beginning to use all this intelligence and shrewdness God had given her. . . . Anna, who had invested her money well and grown richer while all America wallowed in depression and defeat. She was using her brain now for the first time in all her life. The canteen service had begun to grow. There were canteens now in two camps in the Midi and one in the mountains on the Spanish border. Anna somehow had found the workers.

Sometimes in the chilly evenings, when they sat together in the notary's little *salon* with the baby asleep in the next room, they talked, not only about the past but about what was happening day by day. Each day Anna seemed a little more human, a little more free, as if at last the old wounds were healing. She talked of the sort of things she had never before been able to speak of. She told Miss Godwin about the strange distorted life of Paris, with the Ritz and Maxim's filled with Germans and the traitors who worked with them.

"It is a little like Hell," she said, "with the Germans as demons and the others—the double-crossers—as the damned. They are playing a terrible game and are scared all the time that they have picked the wrong cards. If they lose there is only the lamp-post and if they win perhaps only an assassin's bullet."

But they rarely spoke of Jean Pierre Lambert, and then only casually in connection with the baby. Neither of them ever questioned their belief that he would return, although there had been no word of him since he disappeared at Villiers in the long line of refugees moving along the grey and dusty road. Once in the middle of the winter, when Miss Godwin said casually, " Perhaps he is dead or a prisoner," Anna answered, " No, I am sure he is not dead. I am sure he will turn up one day."

She said it with such certainty and vehemence that Miss Godwin looked up from her mending and regarded her with suspicion, as if Anna knew something she had not told her.

But Anna knew nothing at all. It was only her instinct speaking, and perhaps a passionate desire that what she said should be true.

For an extraordinary thing had happened to her. In her mind and spirit, Tom, who had been dead for many years, was no longer dead. He was alive somewhere in the world, the Tom who until now had been the only thing in the world which had ever really mattered to her.

It was a fixation which she herself understood clearly enough, but understanding it did not alter or weaken the conviction. The image of the two men had been blurred, because she in her heart willed it. She did not pretend to herself that she had fallen in love with a man whom she had seen but once in the midst of confusion and terror. It was not like that ; it was simply as if the man had become desirable because, in the emotion and terror of crisis, he had seemed to transport her back into the only real happiness she had ever known. It was all confused and yet remarkably clear. I think that towards the end the identification became complete. Save in her conscious, thinking mind the two men became but one—a Tom-Jean Pierre who had always been hers, even before she was born.

He had reappeared out of the darkness that terrible night among the refugees along the road outside Villiers. He had gone away again, down the same grey road to lose himself among the refugees going south, but he would return again one day. Of that she was certain. It was a kind of madness with her. Whatever there had been in Jean Pierre Lambert, *Capitaine Onzième Sapeurs*, that was unlike Tom was slowly forgotten. The image which remained was that of Tom himself, a little older, Tom as he would have been if he had lived. When she thought of Jean Pierre Lambert, or when Miss Godwin spoke of him or Madame Ritz asked, " Has the father returned yet?" the image she saw was not Jean Pierre Lambert but Tom Harrigan. In some strange fashion Jean Pierre Lambert had *become* Tom Harrigan.

Whatever she did now was for his sake. Jean Pierre Lambert, like Tom and herself, had always been a refugee, an outsider, belonging nowhere. And now with all her money and her wits, she had great power. She could help others like herself and them. That was all that mattered to her.

I think it was as simple as that. It seemed so when Anna told me the curious story.

And slowly during that first winter in Gerbevilliers the baby was becoming her baby, the baby who had died long ago while she worked to support it. It was as if she herself had gone back over all the barren years when she had not lived at all. That, more than any other thing, accounted for the change in her, the change which Miss Godwin found so mysterious. This new Anna was almost happy, with a happiness Miss Godwin had never seen in her before.

On those visits to Paris Anna sometimes had a room on the Cambon side of the Ritz and sometimes in a pinch she had only one of the two tiny bedrooms in the little suite of Madame Ritz under the high mansard on the garden side.

On her second visit to Paris, Von Kleist turned up again.

She met him in the corridor, coming towards her, lean and straight and rather bony in his field-grey uniform.

She had not seen him since that time in Monte Carlo when Miss Godwin and I had dined together and *The Times* had sent for me to go to Germany. She recognized him before he saw her, and in the second or two before they spoke, her mind said to her, " This is your man. Be nice to him. God has sent him to you." For already it was beginning to be difficult, even with all her money, to buy the things she wanted or needed.

At the moment of recognition the smile on his face betrayed his pleasure. He clicked his heels and bowed and said, " I was just thinking of you this afternoon. I heard for the first time that you were still in France. You must have a cocktail with me."

She thought quickly. "I must do it even though people will say I am a collaborationist. Anyway it can be no worse than it is." She was beginning to learn what she must do.

They had cocktails on the Vendôme side in the long wide

hallway, and she learned among other things that he was stationed in Paris, that he was a colonel and that he was important in the administration of the conquered city. Also he lived in the Ritz.

He said, smiling his tired cynical smile, "I heard what you are doing. You American women are very odd. All this is none of your business. Why do you care so much what is happening to these people? Why are a lot of miserable refugees of any concern to you? You are the last person in the world I would have thought of as running a canteen."

She only said, "I am interested in it. It gives me something to do."

"You are a fascinating woman and extremely unpredictable."

She liked the flattery although she knew through long experience that it was only a part of an ancient technique which had become old-fashioned even before the war. That it came from a perfectly experienced and worldly man made it the more palatable.

Then they talked idly for a while of the old days in London, in Monte Carlo and in Paris. She had a strange feeling that they were talking about another world that neither of them would ever see again, as fantastic as this great lounge with Germans sitting everywhere.

Then he asked, "Do you come often to Paris?"

"When I have to come to get money or supplies."

"That must be a little difficult nowadays."

"Yes. More difficult all the time."

"I might be able to help you."

"I will call on you, if I may, when the time comes."

"It would give me pleasure. . . . And will you dine with me and go to the theatre to-night?"

She considered the invitation for a second and then answered, "Yes."

She left him then and went to the sitting-room of Madame Ritz. The old lady was alone with her canaries and Pekinese. It was quite dark and the black-out curtains were drawn across the windows.

Over another cocktail she told Madame Ritz of her meeting with Von Kleist and asked, "Do you think it wise of me to dine with him? It is very difficult to think of him as an enemy. I hate the Germans as a whole. I even hate special Germans like

Von Ribbentrop, but it is difficult to hate someone whom you rather liked, who has always been friendly and flattering."

The old lady poked the little fire and said, " I know how it is. I once thought there were good Germans. Perhaps there still are. I have seen none lately. But my advice would be to be agreeable to him. He is in a position of great power. You might be able to use him. It is all right if you do not mind what people will say of you now and afterwards in the outside world. It may be that some day you will need him desperately."

Anna thought for a moment. " I don't know. Sometimes I can't believe that it will ever be over or that there will ever be any other world. The only world I can believe in is the one I am in now."

Madame Ritz looked at her shrewdly, " What does he want of *you* ? "

" Nothing at all, I should think."

" He has never made love to you ? "

" No . . . save in what he said. He is a peculiar, cold man . . . unlike any man I have ever known. I should think he was unhappy."

" Many Germans are like that. They are the ones who were not meant by God to be Germans."

That wasn't the only day on which Madame Ritz gave her advice. In the little rooms under the mansard with the white curtains and the pots of flowers, Madame Ritz told her many things. It was in a way as if the old lady sat in the centre of a web, a wise spider, knowing everything, aware when the most remote and delicate strand of the web was touched by something. She knew exactly whom to see in order to get a concession. She knew the history of every French collaborator, all their past treacheries, their past mistresses. She knew many strange things which could, if necessary, be used as blackmail. There were things which had come to her during half a century out of the web of hotels that extended over half the earth. Olivier and Frank and Victor and all the rest downstairs had seen things happen, listened to strange conversations on telephones, over-heard snatches of strange talk, seen people go into and come out of rooms unknown to the rest of the world. To the world of service there were few secrets.

In the little room under the mansard she told Anna many of these things. " I have never written them," she said. " I would not have dared to put them on paper lest someone should find them and read them."

Listening, Anna thought, " There is no one alive who knows better the history of all the rottenness which will have to be purged." Perhaps that was what was happening now in all the tragedy and treachery and viciousness. Perhaps in the end the people, in desperation, would arise and destroy their betrayers and exploiters.

One day Madame Ritz said, " You must not think of this war or even the last one as a thing apart. They are all part of something much greater which I shall never live to see the end of and even you may not. It is a part of a revolution going on all over the world—in China, in India, in Russia, even in your country. For thousands of years the human race has been raising itself by its bootstraps and each time it raises itself a little higher. But the process is sometimes evil and bitter."

There were times now when the old woman seemed to be very tired. " It is not easy," she said, " to be decent to people you hold in contempt. I have practised it for many years for the sake of the hotel, for the whole concern. But it is not easy, especially when you are old."

In the little *salon* of the notary's house, Anna told Miss Godwin a lot of the stories Madame Ritz had told her, and this too made Miss Godwin's life more exciting. It gave her the feeling of being on the inside of things.

I was in London during the blitz. It was an unreal, terrifying world like that one used to read about in the more sensational Sunday supplements of American papers, like the things H. G. Wells used to describe in his early novels. Before the blitz people said and wrote that planes would make an end to all war because the civilian population could not endure the horrors of bombing from the air ; but these people were neither very intelligent nor very imaginative, for they underestimated the incredible resilience of the human race.

For weeks we lived in a disintegrating city. It was not like Paris, disintegrating morally, which was worse and more unendurable ; in London it was a physical disintegration. Houses, blocks of flats, churches and hotels were there one day and on the next there would be only a hole in the earth and a heap of rubble with A.R.P. men and firemen digging for the buried dead. And on the night the City burned all the sky was lighted by flames which seemed to lick the clouds from which destruction fell. There was a magnificence not only in the spectacle itself but in the endurance of the people themselves which none who failed to witness it can ever wholly understand or even imagine.

It was all a very long way from that pleasant soft summer night when I walked home from Anna's party.

There were few people in London who hadn't a job to do. Those few weren't wanted and few who did not have to stay chose to remain. I am talking, of course, of that world which had gone to Anna's party, of which the dinner at Ruby Hillyer's was a sample. The poor remained because they could not run away and because the poor are always more attached to the hovels they call home than the rich man to his great house.

Lady Haddonfield and her meek husband, the Marquess, had long since disappeared into obscurity.

They had been too friendly with the Germans, always repeating, "The Germans are very like us . . . much more than the French are." They had done too much entertaining of Germans, had been too friendly with Ribbentrop, had said too often, "It's to our interest to get on with Hitler." After thousands of English citizens had been killed and a quarter of London destroyed, there was not much place left in England for people who once had said, "The Germans are at heart a nice, kind people." Haddonfield House, where I had seen Anna and Lady Haddonfield queening it at the top of the great stairway, was closed and boarded-up, and all the pictures and tapestries were removed to the country, and no one heard much of the Haddonfields. But one rumour I heard was that Lady Haddonfield scarcely remembered Mrs. Bolton. Now that Anna was no longer in London with her contributions of twenty thousand a year for Lady Haddonfield's charities, she was no longer important.

Those who remained in London sometimes met in little groups in hotels or at houses like Ruby Hillyer's. The handsome house in Hill Street was gone and Ruby carried on in a little house in Lord North Street until that was nearly destroyed on the night the Germans bombed the House of Commons. The old world of Anna's party was pretty well dissipated. Some of the people in that world remained what they had been—idle, trivial, useless

and a little vicious. Some of them, lost and despairing, did away
with themselves. And a few of them discovered out of the agony
of the times a new and unsuspected life of usefulness and decency
which both astonished and satisfied them.

One day, at a small luncheon at Ruby's, one of them asked,
" Whatever became of Anna Bolton ? " Someone else said, " I
hear she stayed behind and is in Paris now." One, a little more
vicious, said, " I hear she is a collaborationist. She's living in
Vichy and spends a great deal of time in Paris dining with
Germans at Maxim's and the Ritz."

Ruby remained loyal. She said, " That's not at all the story
I heard. It came to me from a friend in Geneva—a journalist
who has been in Paris. I hear she is giving everything she has for
the refugees and the people in concentration camps. I hear she's
doing a great work."

But that only gave rise to a bitter witticism from one of the
sexless men who was working at the Ministry of Information.
He said, " Yes, I heard that she had given her last exercise
mattress to help the refugees."

But no one really knew what had become of Anna, myself
least of all. She had simply disappeared after the Germans went
into Paris, and in London the memory of her wealth, her parties,
her jewels and furs was rapidly becoming a legend of that world
which had vanished for ever with the blitz. Sitting there at
Ruby's table, talking about Anna and that dead world, was like
talking of something out of the eighteenth century. Too many
things had happened, too many incredible things, since Ruby
had left the house in Hill Street. To all of us then, Anna was to
all intents and purposes dead, a legendary character.

But this is Anna's story, not mine. I left London for Cairo
and presently went to Singapore and Sydney. I heard no more
of her, save that now and then I encountered someone who
asked, " What became of Anna Bolton ? "

In Gerbevilliers she had become used to the ugly, uncomfortable little house of the notary. She stayed there because it was
convenient, and after a time she and Miss Godwin became even
fond of the house with its dreary wallpaper and the ornate ugly
furniture of the little *salon*. It came to have the look of home,
with knitting lying on the table, and the nappies of the baby
drying in the little garden by the river, and one corner of the
room usually stacked high with cases of chocolates or cigarettes

or bandages. Happiness can transform a house just as living in a house can transform it, and Anna and Miss Godwin were happy there, in spite of worries, of discomforts, of all the misery which surrounded them. For food was beginning to be scarce, even in a provincial town like Gerbevilliers. There was no butter and no cream and very little fresh milk. For herself and Miss Godwin it did not matter. For herself it mattered even less than for Miss Godwin, since she was young and strong, and when she went to Paris and dined at Maxim's she had every sort of luxurious food—even *langouste* and caviare and *pâté de foie gras*. The Germans saw to that.

In spite of her contentment and the excitement of her work, Miss Godwin looked much older, and the skin seemed drawn more tightly across the high distinguished cheekbones. Her veined, delicate hands, which had never before done any work, were coarse and red and chapped.

Usually when she came down from the brickyard, she was talkative and almost gay, as if she were wound up to the breaking-point by long hours and overwork. Anna began to watch her slyly without Miss Godwin noticing it, wondering whether she ought not to send her out of all this and back to America. She had never talked about going home because she had not dared to think of Miss Godwin leaving her. It was now almost as if Miss Godwin had taken the place of Mary Scanlon, the charwoman, as if she had become Anna's own mother. And she could not contemplate what would become of the baby if Miss Godwin were not there.

And then one night when Miss Godwin came down from the brickyard, she took off her coat and hat, sat down in front of the *salamandre* and began to cry. When Anna found her there, she knelt beside her and put her arms about her. For a long time she let her cry and said nothing at all. Presently she said, " Tell me. What is it ? "

Miss Godwin blew her nose and said, " I'm sorry to be such a fool. I'm sorry to drivel like this. It's only because Ernst died this afternoon."

Anna could not think at first who Ernst was, for she had less time for the brickyard than Miss Godwin and knew the people less intimately. When she asked, Miss Godwin answered, " It was the Austrian boy from Innsbruck—the one who had tuberculosis. You see, he asked especially for me. Four of the others gave up their chocolate to bribe a guard to come down and tell me. I only got there in time."

She leaned across the table and picked up her heavy leather handbag and opened it, taking out a piece of coarse paper. She handed it silently to Anna.

"You see," she said, "he gave me that, with the names of his mother and sister in Innsbruck. He told me what to write them. He had not heard from them for nearly two years." She began to cry again. "He was so young," she said, "and he wanted to live. He shouldn't have died."

Anna read the names on the paper. "I can get a message to them. I can send them some money. Von Kleist can arrange it for me. There are so many people to-day who shouldn't die."

After supper the baby crawled about the floor for a time and even walked a little way hanging on to Anna's finger. He looked fat and his cheeks were pink and his eyes bright. He made gurgling sounds and little grunts as if he were trying to talk. When he grew tired, Anna picked him up and held him in her arms until he fell asleep.

When she had put him to bed, she returned to the little *salon*. The sight of the baby had changed Miss Godwin's mood and she was sitting by the little stove sewing a nightgown she was making for him. Long ago, as part of her training as a lady, Miss Godwin had learned the art of hemstitching and embroidery, and she was making the nightgown an elegant affair with the baby's name "Jean Pierre" embroidered in blue silk across the chest. It made Anna want to laugh, but she gave no sign of her amusement and went to work on her account books.

Presently, when she was tired, she said, "There's something I've wanted to speak about for a long time. I should have spoken about it earlier but I couldn't do it, somehow. It's about you. You ought to have a rest. You look tired and ill."

But Miss Godwin ignored the idea. "It's nothing at all to worry about," she said. "I've always been like this since I was a girl . . . up and down. Probably next week I'll be looking fresh as a daisy. I look worse to-night than usual. What happened to-day upset me."

Anna didn't say, "But you are old now—you must be nearly seventy. It won't be up and down any more. All this is too much for you."

That was what, with a feeling of tautness about the heart, she was thinking, but she didn't say it. Instead she said, " That's true. Just the same, all this is too hard for you. You ought to go home and lead a decent quiet life."

Miss Godwin didn't look at her. She only appeared to concentrate more profoundly on the business of embroidering " Jean Pierre " in baby blue on the nightgown.

" This *is* a decent life," she said, almost passionately. " It's the decentest life I've ever had. To-day when he was dying, Ernst sat up, leaned against me and he said, ' Thank you, Mademoiselle, for all you've done. God knows of it. He will not forget ! ' Do you think that wasn't the decentest moment I have ever known ? "

She began to cry again silently, with her head bent, but Anna knew she was crying, for she saw the tears falling on the baby's nightgown.

Anna didn't answer her and she said, " No. I'm not going away. You can't send me. What would I do in New York, sitting there idly, knowing what was going on in the world and me doing nothing about it ? No, I *won't* go away. It doesn't matter what happens to an old woman like me."

Anna said, " You are very stubborn."

" And what would you do without me, and what would the baby do ? "

" That's not important."

And then she saw that Miss Godwin had been hurt by the suggestion that she go away. A great wave of warmth swept over her and she heard herself saying, as if another self were speaking, " It seems silly to me that we should go on calling each other ' Mrs. Bolton ' and ' Miss Godwin ' after all this time. From now on I mean to call you Harriette and I hope you'll call me Anna."

Miss Godwin only said, " I've felt the same way, Anna . . . for a long time, only I didn't feel that I was the one to change things."

And then Anna began to cry too, not from sadness but out of weariness and an immense sudden gratitude towards Miss Godwin, towards the baby, towards Jean Pierre Lambert and the dead girl lying on the floor of the Mairie her head propped against a law book, towards old Madame Ritz, towards all those who had helped her or been kind to her. It was an extraordinary sensation, as if something inside her head burst, as if at last she were whole, as if never again would she be hurt or afraid, as if never again would it be necessary " to show Lewisburg." Somehow for the first time in all her life she knew what friendship and love for another woman could be ; for even her mother, Mary Scanlon, she had never loved because Mary Scanlon had never allowed herself to be loved. She had always acted as if her daughter Anna was something wonderful and shining, a being apart from her whom she might worship but never touch. She had always been a servant to her own child.

Sitting there in the dreary little *salon* of the dead notary's house, Anna was suddenly free.

It happened the next afternoon while Miss Godwin was attending the burial of the Austrian boy Ernst. He was buried in the little graveyard outside the concentration camp among forty-seven other lonely refugees who had grown tired of life and were buried there. Miss Godwin arranged the service with the village priest. In order that it should seem a little less lonely she persuaded the wife of the Mayor and Madame St. Genis, the baker's wife, to go with her, and together the three women stood in the slow drizzle of rain beside the grave while the priest read the service.

Anna stayed at home with the baby, finishing the inventory of supplies that grew a little smaller each week as it became more and more difficult to find cocoa and tinned milk and cigarettes and other things. As she worked the falling mist outside the windows of the little *salon* blurred all the landscape, so that the outlines of the distant poplars and the forest itself seemed vague and hazy like a Corot picture. It was a soothing day, for Anna loved greenness and dampness and the sound of the water falling over the weir at the end of the garden.

She had been working for a long time, until her eyes grew tired, and leaning back in her chair she looked out of the window across the garden. At the same moment she saw something which caused her to sit upright and stare.

On the opposite side of the little river, just below the weir a man was fishing. He was dressed in an old jacket with riding breeches tucked into high leather boots. He wore an old felt hat and over his shoulder carried a creel. She thought, " It's Tom ! "

It was Tom exactly as he had been long ago, in the days before they were married, when sometimes they drove into the mountains of West Virginia to fish. Many times she had seen him thus, balancing himself on strong, widely spread legs as he cast the line over the water. For a moment she was no longer in France at all but back in West Virginia hills and Tom was not dead but standing there on the opposite side of the little river.

Then she thought, "I am going mad ! The whole thing is becoming an obsession." She rose, a little frightened, and walked to the window. The likeness of the figure on the opposite bank of the river to Tom still remained but the outline became no clearer in the falling mist. It was all soft and blurred and in the fading light the figure was almost ghostlike.

She felt a sudden impulse to go to the door, open it, run to the end of the garden, and call out to the stranger. But it passed quickly as impossible and silly. And then while she stood there, the man reeled in his line, bent his head low over the wet fly to examine it, turned suddenly and walked along the river out of sight beyond the garden wall.

It was the walk she recognized, and the recognition made her understand the sudden feeling of Tom's presence. It was the walk of Jean Pierre Lambert, *Capitaine of the Onzième Sapeurs*, as he went down the dusty road in the early morning light to disappear among the crowd of dusty refugees.

Standing there, staring out of the window but seeing nothing, she was certain now that she had not been wrong. It *was* the Captain. She thought, "I am not crazy. I really saw him. That is who it is." But what was he doing in Gerbevilliers ? Why hadn't he come at once to the house to see the baby ? What did it mean ?

She turned away from the window, feeling an extraordinary sense of exultation. She was not mad ! "What I saw was true ! I was not wrong in believing he was so like Tom !" And even now, when she thought of the Captain, it was really Tom she saw.

It was late when Miss Godwin, looking tired and grey, came in from the funeral. She noticed the excitement in Anna, that her eyes were bright and her colour high, but Anna betrayed nothing. The cook laid supper on the table and the baby sat with them in his high chair, healthy and good as always. After supper Anna put the baby to bed and returned to the *salon* to read one of the novels of Balzac which she had borrowed from the library of Monseigneur Dubois.

Miss Godwin finished hemstitching "Jean Pierre's" nightgown and said, "I think I'll go to bed now." She kissed Anna lightly on the cheek and went up the narrow stairs to her bedroom. Looking after her, Anna thought, "She looks more pale and tired every day . . . maybe worse to-day because of Ernst's funeral."

How long afterwards the tap came on the door she did not know, for she was lost in the Balzac story—willingly lost to forget many things. She was indeed so lost that she did not hear the first tap but only when it was repeated. It did not startle her. Quite often people came late at night when there was illness in the town because the medicines they needed could no longer be found at *pharmacies*. And Anna had never had any physical fear, perhaps because the inner hurt and fear had always been so much greater than any physical fear could be.

He was standing there when she opened the door, so big that he seemed to fill all the doorway. Again for a moment she had a sense of hallucination. But he spoke to her almost at once in his deep warm voice.

"I'm sorry to have come so late. I would not have knocked but I saw light between the shutters."

"It doesn't matter. I never go to bed early."

She stood aside for him to come in, aware that she was trembling, thinking, "I must not make a fool of myself."

It was still raining and his coat and hat were wet, not as if he had walked only a little way but as if he had been walking for hours in the rain. He was no longer in the fishing costume but wore a cheap, rather shabby blue suit, a blue shirt and a cheap raincoat.

"Put your coat there by the stove."

"Thank you," he said quite simply and hung his coat over a chair. It was as if he too were aware of the curious sense of strain. It seemed to her that she really saw him clearly for the first time by the lamplight—the heavy shoulders, the high cheekbones, the flat cheeks with the high colour, and the curly black hair.

"The baby," he said, "how is he?"

She smiled, "He is wonderful. He's grown so much that

you won't know him. He's right here in the next room. He sleeps in my room. When I'm away Miss Godwin sleeps in my bed."

" Does he talk ? "

Again she smiled. " He makes sounds. He's really too young to talk."

A little sadly he said, " I've not had much experience with babies." In his voice, in what he said, there was a curious echo of feeling as if he were thinking, " If there had been no war, if she had not died, I could have had a home. I could have known my son."

Quietly she said, " Come. We'll look at him." And picking up the lamp she led the way into her bedroom.

There in his crib, in one of the nightgowns Miss Godwin had made for him, the baby lay on his stomach, his head dark against the pillow. Together they stood beside the crib while she held the lamp.

Over the Captain's face came an extraordinary look of tenderness, and she knew suddenly that he was thinking of the girl who lay dead in the Mairie at Villiers. His hand reached out gently towards the child and she knew what it was he wanted.

She said, " Would you like to hold him ? "

He looked towards her and smiled, " Yes."

It was bad to waken the baby, but it did not matter. It was impossible to resist the hungry look in the Captain's eyes. For a moment it was exactly as if Tom had come in late from the office in the little flat back in Pittsburgh, and stood with her beside the baby's crib.

Gently she lifted the child and put him in the Captain's arms. The baby opened its eyes and yawned and then smiled at him.

She said, " I think he knows you. He is a very good baby."

Then he held the child up so that its face touched his own. With one hand the baby pulled at his hair. Then after a moment he sighed and said, " I suppose he should go back to sleep."

He gave the baby back to her and she laid him in the crib.

" I think if we leave him he'll go back to sleep."

Then she picked up the lamp and led the way back into the little *salon*. There she put the lamp on the table and said, " I'll get some wine and biscuits."

" That will be good."

"Sit down there and put your feet near the stove. Your boots are very wet."

He obeyed her like a child and when she returned he was sitting with his elbows on his knees, his head in his hands. She was aware that something was troubling him. For a moment he sat as if he were unaware of her presence. Then he turned towards her and smiled. It was the first time she had ever seen him really smile.

"It's very good of you," he said, taking the wine.

They raised their glasses and drank. Then he said, "You don't think anyone saw me come here?"

"No. It's unlikely. They go to sleep a little after sundown in Gerbevilliers . . . now that there's no gas or electricity and oil is hard to get."

"I would have come earlier but I was afraid of being seen coming here. Some day it might make trouble for you."

She did not ask him why. Instead she said, "I saw you on the river bank. Why didn't you come in then?"

"I wanted everything to appear usual and in order. I am staying here with my uncle, St. Genis."

She looked at him in surprise. How could he, a Russian refugee from the last war, have an uncle who was a French baker living in a provincial town like Gerbevilliers? The obvious lie made her wince with mistrust.

He was smiling a slow, humorous smile which said, "Of course he isn't really my uncle. I'm only pretending that for a reason."

Then he continued, "I wanted the town to be used to me. Nowadays, if a stranger entered a town like this and simply walked into a house and walked off with a baby, it would arouse curiosity and perhaps make a great deal of trouble.

As she listened to him, she felt suddenly cold and faint. Very quietly she said, "You are not going to take the baby away?"

"That is why I came."

"You can't do that! You haven't any place to take him. You wouldn't be able to get the right kind of milk! You couldn't take him away. It would be very bad for him."

He seemed astonished by her display of emotion. "I have found a place for him. I think I could find milk."

"It isn't only that. There are so many other things. He's used to me now. Don't you see, I can give him things no one else can give him."

He looked away from her as if he did not want to pain her.
" I have thought it out. I think it is best."

" But why ? He's in the country here. He has good air and
good food."

For a moment he was silent. He put down his glass and lighted
a cigarette. Then he said, " You have been very good to me and
to the baby. I am grateful for that. I think it would be better
for the baby, for you and for me that we settle the thing now."

" But why ? "

She was aware now that it was not only that she could not bear
the loss of the baby, but that if she lost the baby she would probably never see him again. It was very clear to her now that without knowing it she had in a way fallen in love with this man
whom she had seen but once before in all her life. Inside she felt
confused and terrified by all the elements which seemed mixed
up in the thing ; even that new sense of freedom and her love
for Miss Godwin had something to do with it. She felt panic
and hysteria rising in her. The Captain was leaning forward
now and holding his cigarette between his thumb and forefinger
as Tom had always done.

Very gravely he said, " You see, Madame, we are on different
sides of the fence. I have no friends among the Germans or the
collaborateurs. I wouldn't want the little one corrrupted, and it
makes it very dangerous for me and for yourself. I am dangerous
to you and you are dangerous to me."

So that was it !

Then he said, " You see, we know a great deal."

" But I have to do what I'm doing," she said. " I have to do
it to get all the things I need. I have to do it in order to go back
and forth freely across the line. If I didn't see those people I
shouldn't be able to help all the refugees, all the wretched people
up there in the brickyard."

He was watching her coldly, judging her.

" Is that why you do it ? Are you speaking the truth ? "

" I swear it on the head of my mother. If it is not true I pray
to God to strike me dead as I sit in this chair. I hate all those
people, the *collaborateurs* and the Boches. I hate them all passionately." She knew now that she spoke the truth. It was the
first time she had spoken it. She hated them all . . . all those
people who came between her and the baby . . . and the man
sitting opposite her. She had not really known it until now.

[110]

He did not answer her at once. He sat quite still, looking at her directly out of the clear, honest blue eyes. Her own eyes met his without quavering.

" You believe me, don't you ? "

" I don't know," he said slowly. " It's so hard in these times to believe anybody." Then he added, " It is puzzling, though, that you should do so much for the refugees and the poor fellows in the camps. It is difficult to explain . . . hard to know which side to believe."

He was wrestling with the problem, seeking, just as Tom had always done, to solve it by sheer brute force and strength.

Quietly she said, " I doubt that you know how much the baby means to me, how much I want to do for him. It isn't only now . . . but afterwards when things are settled." Almost with shame, she said, " I am a very rich woman."

" I guessed that, but that is not the reason for my listening to you. Money could spoil the boy. It could give him the wrong philosophy of life."

For a long time in the back of her mind an impulse had been lingering, and now it was born. Again, as if she were swept away despite herself, she said, " I haven't always been rich. My mother was a *femme de ménage*, my father a *petit fonctionnaire*. Don't think I don't understand how wretched it is to be poor, and how evil a thing riches can be if you do not know how to use them."

" I'm thinking all the time about the boy," he said. " If anything should happen to me. It could happen any time."

A chill passed over her but she managed to say, " If anything should happen to you, I would see to it that he was educated and well trained in whatever you like."

" I should like him to be an engineer. There will be so much building to be done after this is over. There are things which worry me. My father was a White Russian, a court official, a refugee. He was a good man but he was very wrong about Russia. I want the boy to be prepared for a new world —not a dead world." His wide brow was creased with the effort of his thinking. It seemed to her that he was talking as if he were already dead.

" If you will listen for a moment I will tell you a story and then maybe you will believe me."

" I will listen."

Then she told him as quickly as possible the whole story, going back all the way to the High School in Lewisburg. She told him everything about Tom and Ezra Bolton and how she hired Miss Godwin. She told him everything up to the curious scene with Miss Godwin when something inside her seemed to burst and she was set free. If that had not happened she could not have talked to the Captain as she was now talking. It was the first time she had ever told the whole story. She abased herself, suffered agonies of shame, but she played for great stakes.

He listened, scarcely moving the whole time.

When she had finished, she said, " That is how it is. That is the truth."

" I will leave the boy with you," he said. " I think you understand things. I think *she* would like it this way." He smiled at her. " Shall we have another drink ? "

This time he poured the wine and as he stood, he raised his glass and said, " To your good work, Madame." They drank and she raised her glass. " To the future of the boy. May he become a great engineer."

She had won and now she wanted to turn completely feminine and burst into tears. It was not only from relief but from the sense of something that had happened between her and the Captain. They were friends, perhaps more than friends. This was no longer the man who had slapped her face and then treated her politely but with contempt. There was a warmth and understanding between them that had not been there before. She thought, " I am only beginning to live now. I dare not cry. It would be cheap and indecent."

She managed to say, " We did not know the boy's name. We call him Jean . . . Jean Pierre, after you."

" That is what we had planned to call him . . . Jean . . . Jean Pierre."

Then he stood up and said, " We have talked a long time. I apologize. I must go now. There is something I must do before daylight."

She said, " Would you like to look at him . . . without waking him again ? "

" Yes." He spoke almost shyly now.

She picked up the lamp and they went again to stand over the crib looking down at the sleeping child. This time they did not waken him and when they came out of the room Lambert walked over and picked up his coat.

"I have been here so long that my coat is nearly dry." Then he laughed. "It is lucky the neighbours go to bed early or there'd be a scandal going about the town to-morrow."

At the door he turned and with his hand on the knob said, "You have been very good to me, Madame, and to the little one."

She wanted to cry out, "Don't go! Don't go!" There was still so much they had to tell each other.

"It's nothing," she said. "The baby is worth it all and more. He has made a great difference to me." There was a little awkward silence and she said, "Will I hear from you?"

"I won't write. I have no address. And it might be disagreeable or dangerous for you. I will come back when I can. It's well established now that I'm Monsieur St. Genis's nephew." After a second he added, "He is one of us."

And then she knew that he really believed all she had told him and that he trusted her. A thought came to her suddenly and she said, "Wait!" He looked at her curiously while she picked up the lamp and went into the bedroom.

In a moment she returned, carrying a whole sheaf of thousand franc notes. She held them towards him and said, "Take this. It will help."

The colour came into his face. "I couldn't do that, Madame. I couldn't take money. . . ."

"It's not for you. It's for what you are doing."

He smiled, "In that case . . ." Then he took her hand and kissed it, very quietly and with dignity, and looked at her curiously. "You are a very remarkable woman. Things happen in the most extraordinary ways . . . that we should have met thus on the road outside Villiers! Good-night and God's blessing on you and your work."

Then he was gone, closing the door behind him. Outside the rain had stopped and the moon was shining.

For a moment she leaned against the table smiling to herself and then, pouring herself a glass of wine, she sat down again by the stove to think, still smiling. It was nearly dawn when she at last went to bed and fell asleep.

When she wakened, Miss Godwin had already gone out and the baby was in the little *salon*, playing in the pen made out of packing-cases, while the cook looked in now and then to see if he was all right. At first everything that had happened the night before had the dreamlike quality of something she had imagined, just as she had imagined many times what it would be like when he came back. Lately the line between reality and what she dreamed, especially here in Gerbevilliers, had been very thin. Now she had almost a belief that Tom had not died at all, but somehow had come back last night to see her. For an instant she thought, " Maybe nothing happened at all last night. Maybe I only dreamed it. Maybe I am going crazy."

But when she came into the little *salon* the bottle of wine and the wine-glasses were still on the table and a pair of worn, heavy leather gloves lying on the floor near the stove. She thought, remembering his appearance the night before, " It is too bad he forgot them. He will need them. He is very poor." And then it came back to her that she had given him all the money she had in the house—more than fifteen thousand francs which the Germans, perhaps Von Kleist himself, had got through from Switzerland ; and she smiled at the thought that now she was a part of the Underground because she had given to the Captain money which the Germans themselves had got for her.

Then quickly, almost secretly, she picked up the gloves and carried them into her room where she put them among the handkerchiefs in the top drawer of the dressing-table. There was something about the gloves that was extraordinarily like him. They gave her a sense of security and pleasure.

At lunch time Miss Godwin returned and when she glanced at Anna there was a look of hurt in her eyes, as if she knew Anna was hiding something from her.

Anna closed the door leading into the kitchen and said, " He came back last night."

" Who ? " asked Miss Godwin.

" Jean's father."

" I noticed the glasses on the table and the gloves."

" I didn't call you because I thought you needed the sleep. I thought you would see him to-day. I only found out as he left that he was not coming back."

Miss Godwin, she knew, did not believe her and she was still hurt, and Anna, ashamed, thought, " I behaved like a child—

like a girl of eighteen in love. I wanted him for myself." If Miss Godwin had been there everything would have been different—no more than a visit from a stranger. There would only have been formality with no understanding between them.

While they ate lunch she told Miss Godwin all that had happened, even about giving him the money, and Miss Godwin, in her interest, forgot that she had been cheated out of seeing the good-looking Captain. But Anna could see that she was still suspicious of the reasons why she had not wakened her.

The next day when Anna left for Paris, Miss Godwin had not quite forgiven her. There was a faint chill over the parting which left a cloud of depression over her during all the journey in the crowded, evil-smelling train.

It seemed to her that each trip she made to Paris the train became a little dirtier, a little more crowded, the faces of her fellow-travellers a little more pinched and transparent. It was as if one saw in the trains in miniature a whole country falling into despair and apathy. Many of the passengers looked as ill as the men and women in the concentration camps.

And Paris itself was no better. It was like a ghost city with empty streets and citizens who stared suspiciously at you as you passed. She found a horse-drawn cab at the Gare d'Orsay and drove through the twilight across the river to the Ritz. In the blue darkness, the great bulk of the dark, deserted Louvre gave the impression of a dead palace inhabited only by ghosts. The arches of the Rue de Rivoli and the Rue Castiglione were dark save for tiny blue lights. Now and then a figure appeared for an instant in an archway and then vanished again.

At the hotel there was a message for her from Madame Ritz. Could she come to her apartment? There was an important message.

The old lady was wearing a dressing-gown and dining in her room. She looked very old and tired, with no make-up and dark circles about her eyes. The two Pekinese sat on chairs beside her. The canary cages were covered with pieces of purple brocade.

When she had ordered a cocktail for Anna and made a little conversation about the journey, she said, "There is bad news. They have begun to shoot hostages to end the sabotage !"

At first Anna thought dully, "How stupid ! It won't do any good."

And then suddenly it became a personal thing which touched her with horror. He was working in the Underground. If they caught him, it would happen to him. It was even worse than if he were French by birth. A Russian they would hate viciously.

"They shot fifty innocent men to-day," said Madame Ritz. "You see, they are not like other people. They are different from any people in Europe. It would be better if they were out-and-out barbarians like some of the Balkan people, instead of being just brutes with the pretence of being civilized."

Anna did not say anything and the old lady went on, "I advise you to go away now while you can. Everything is closing in—I know how you have been getting money, but even that isn't going to last much longer. You're in a bad position, my dear Anna. You're neither one thing nor the other. You play with the collaborators and help the refugees. Neither side really trusts you. It's a dangerous business. There is a time coming when neither side will ask questions or look for justifications. They'll simply kill those they cannot be sure of."

"I can't go away," said Anna dully, "I can't."

Madame Ritz shrugged her shoulders. She glanced at Anna, raised her coffee cup to her lips, drank and put it down. "There is another thing you must remember. If anything happens to me, it will be much more difficult for you. Heaven knows what would happen here in this hotel. It's been very convenient for you, because they trust me. I've never meddled openly in anything. It's covered up a lot of things for you. I'm not going to live for ever—especially in these times."

Anna said, "I'll think about it. Perhaps you are right."

Madame Ritz reached across the table and touched her hand. "You must remember one thing, Anna—that when the money is gone and you can't get any more, you are nobody, just like all the rest. There'll be nothing to protect you. There'll be no special privileges."

"I'll think it over. I'll consider it carefully."

"There isn't much time. It will happen more and more quickly now. Get out! It is the only thing to do."

Get out! She couldn't get out now. She couldn't go away not knowing where he was or what had become of him. It would be better to die than to go on for ever not knowing.

The death of Tom had been bad enough, but that was sharp and clean and final. She couldn't go through this twice in a lifetime. A kind of wavering anguish seized her. It passed quickly and left her thinking, " But I am a fool. I don't even know whether he is even friendly towards me, whether he thinks of me except with contempt." But quickly he seemed very near to her, here beside her in Madame Ritz's little cottage high up above the garden. It was a quick, vivid sensation, very real, such as had never occurred to her before, even with Tom. Yet somehow he was Tom.

She heard Madame Ritz saying, " Something has happened to you since I saw you last."

She had to pull herself together. She said quickly, " No, nothing. Nothing that I can think of. I'm a little tired."

" It isn't that at all. No, it's different." Then she said suddenly, " I've never asked you about the baby's father. Did he ever return ? "

" He came back two days ago."

For a little while Madame Ritz didn't say anything. Then she said, " Then I was wrong about him. I am glad I was wrong. I'm always glad when the human race turns out better than one expects." That was all she said but Anna knew that she understood the whole thing.

Then she said, " Colonel Von Kleist wants you to dine with him the first night you are in Paris. It is about something important. I don't know what. He has not asked you to marry him ? "

" No."

Madame Ritz smiled, " On both sides there are men who want to play both ends against the middle. It would be no disadvantage to have a rich wife with all her money invested in gilt-edged shares in America. When the war is over, investments elsewhere won't amount to much . . . not even foreign currency . . . no matter who wins. And whatever happens, an American wife will be an asset. I don't mean to disparage your other qualities, you understand ? "

" I've no illusions," said Anna.

Anna dined with Colonel Von Kleist that night at Maxim's.

She dressed carefully, feeling by instinct that it was necessary that she should look her best. There were no jewels ; they were locked away. But she wore a black and silver dress that showed off her figure to advantage, and artificial pearls, and when she looked at her image in the mirror, she thought, " Annie Scanlon looks distinguished—the way duchesses are supposed to look." But she wasn't very interested any more.

While she dressed she thought a great deal about the Prussian Colonel, considering the speculations of Madame Ritz, wondering at his stupidity—that he thought any American woman in these times would consider marrying a German, much less an independent woman like herself. And then, trying to see the picture from the other side, she understood that very likely he would consider marriage with himself a privilege and an honour, Germans were like that, especially Germans of his class, and their gigantic, bitterly resented sense of inferiority made them worse, more fanatic in their pride. Thinking about it, it seemed to her that all the Germans she had ever known in the Europe of the past few years belonged to two classes—those decadent ones who strove always to lose their nationality and race and merge themselves into the cosmopolitan, international carnival ; or those who kept saying all the time, like children whistling in the dark lane at midnight, " Look at me ! I am a German, of the noblest of races. Why don't you admire and like me ? "

She had no very strong sense of nationality. People with Anna's bitter history are not likely to be stirred by profound feelings of nationalism. Her money came out of America but that was an accident, because an ageing man in the last flare-up of passion had found his secretary necessary to his peace. All the Lewisburg part of her life was bitterness and resentment, all but Tom who had nothing to do with anything. Everything which had happened with Tom was a glorious manifestation of Nature which could have happened anywhere, because Nature is greater than such things as nationality. And even that had ended in tragedy and bitterness, since his people had been ashamed of her because she was poor and her mother was a charwoman. No, she had no great reason to have a strong sense of nationality.

Slowly she had come to think of people as people, regardless of background or colour or race or creed. In a way she was a kind of buccaneer.

And so she did not think of the Colonel as a German with all the prejudices and hatreds she might have felt had she been a more conventional person with a more conventional background. He existed for her as an individual, and as such there were some things she liked in him and many she disliked. She liked his cynical hard sense of humour, and the fatalism which could only exist in a man as hard as himself. She liked his weary, only half-concealed disgust for the Fuehrer and most of the men around him, disgust at their vulgarity, and lack of taste, and noisiness. There were times when she thought that if he had been born elsewhere in the world than in Germany, he might have been a remarkable, perhaps even a great man. But Germany herself had crippled him as it had crippled so many men in her brief history. He was deformed in his sudden half-insane spasms of pride, in his cruelty and coldness, in his sudden bursts of hatred for England because she was rich and powerful, and for France because she was civilized. That he was complex and tortured and at times morbid, she knew well enough. All these things she disliked in him.

Being rich and independent, there was no reason for her to marry save for love and one could not love Von Kleist. With some women he might become an obsession, but it would be impossible to love him, honestly, warmly and decently. If you had loved Tom, so warm and simple and vigorous and tender, you could not love a man like the Colonel. If you had seen the simplicity and directness and warmth of a man like the Captain —no, Von Kleist was for women who were silly idiots or who had strong, depraved tastes.

He was waiting for her in the bar, noisy at this hour and filled with German officers and their women. A few of them were wives ; you could spot them by their scrubbed frumpiness. Even fewer were German mistresses whom you could identify by the fashion in which they were overdressed, wearing too much jewellery, too many furs, too much make-up, now that all Paris lay open to their plundering. One had the impression that they wore two pairs of silk stockings and two hats.

The others were mostly women of uncertain nationality, plying their trade, who had been caught in Paris or flocked there when all Europe collapsed. She thought, " Only a hair separates them from me. They are getting on as best they can. I have money. They have none. When I can no longer get money, what becomes of me ? I shall have to go back to America."

But when she looked at the Colonel she knew she had no intention of going, for the sight of him made her compare him at once with Jean Pierre Lambert standing there beneath the pruned linden trees outside the Mairie at Villiers. The Colonel stood stiff, and straight, and coldly handsome in his grey-green uniform. He was still, as he had been in London years before, neat and clean with the intolerable cleanliness which sometimes afflicts perverse men with whom physical cleanliness is a kind of morbid obsession.

The Captain had stood there looking down at her, stained with blood and dust, wearing an old ill-fitting coat to cover the nakedness left by his torn shirt. Yet there was a magnificence about him, even in the tragedy which had overwhelmed him only a little while before. Even in the cheap blue suit and raincoat as he stood in the doorway of the notary's house he had possessed the same warmth and splendour. There was still enough of Annie Scanlon in Anna Bolton to know when a man was a man.

They walked to Maxim's through the dark streets and all the way the Colonel scarcely spoke. She had the impression that something was troubling him, a curious impression which came to her through the thick darkness.

As they turned into the Rue Royale he said, " I'm tired to-night."

" I'm sorry. Have you been working hard lately ? "

He sighed. " No more than usual. Only it's monotonous. Always doing the same thing—red tape, orders, paper work. And lately the feeling that one can't walk a few yards after dark without the fear of getting a knife in the back."

She did not answer him but she thought again suddenly of Jean Pierre Lambert.

" I'm sick of the whole thing. I don't like Paris like this. I've applied to go to Russia—to the front. Anything is better than this."

Politely she said, " I can understand that."

She wanted to be on the good side of him. There was the question of getting more money through, of getting supplies. If he went away, it might become difficult or impossible. She remembered suddenly the warning and advice of Madame Ritz.

" Everything is getting worse," he said gloomily. And she thought, " Are they all thinking that ? Are they all beginning to doubt ? "

Then they were in front of Maxim's and she stepped into the revolving door, coming suddenly from the darkness of the street into the light of the restaurant.

It was filled with Germans and their women, and it was noisy. It was as if she had not left the bar at the Ritz. Here in Maxim's were the same people. They went back and forth between the two places because in the old days that had been the *chic* thing to do. Only now it was different. The Germans made the difference. Maxim's had lost its quality of brilliance. It was like a German beer garden.

They dined well, for in Maxim's one could have not only all one wanted to eat but one could have caviare and pheasant and *pâté de foie gras* and champagne. She ate it all, greedily, feeling shamefaced yet philosophical. If she did not eat it, the Germans would. It would never get to the refugees and the prisoners, or the millions of people who did not even have bread. And for the first time she realized that for weeks she had really been hungry, that she was eating urgently like a hungry person.

The depression seemed to cling to the Colonel. During all the dinner he did not talk much. The food was good and the crowd was entertaining to watch. At the end they had good brandy, and this and the champagne seemed to loosen the tongue of the Colonel. There was suddenly less of a crowd too and less noise.

They gossiped for a time about the old days and speculated as to whether Paris would ever again be as it had been before the war. There were moments when the Colonel seemed to forget that he was a German, moments when he could seem almost like a Frenchman or an Englishman or an American. It may have been all the years he spent outside Germany before the war that made the difference.

Then he said suddenly, looking at the glass of brandy cupped in his hands, " There is something I wanted to ask you." And Anna thought, " How extraordinary! He's going to do what Madame Ritz said he would do." And in a low voice, she said, " Yes. What is it ? "

" I would like you to marry me." Then he turned and looked at her directly, his face a little softened.

She did not answer him at once, having no words with which to answer. What he said made very little direct impression. She could only consider the unreal quality of the whole scene— that here in Maxim's, in the midst of all that was going on in the world, a man, a German, should be asking her to marry him, not in the headlong fashion of the day, as young people married

[121]

—because there was so little time—but quietly, with dignity and calculation, as if nothing at all were happening, as if the old world had gone on unchanged.

The feel of his eyes staring at her made her uncomfortable and she said, " No . . . I don't think I could do that."

" Why not ? We are both intelligent people—worldly and experienced. We are individualists, above the things which are happening about us."

The remark startled her because she had never considered him as a man who thought thus. She wanted to say, " I am not experienced or worldly at all. I thought I was, but it isn't true. I know nothing at all. I have never been more confused and inexperienced than at this moment.

The very idea of marrying Von Kleist was so preposterous that it was beyond consideration, but she did not want to offend him. There was still too much she had to have from him before the whole story was finished.

" No," she heard herself saying. " You know it is impossible. I'm grateful for all you've done but it's no good. It's impossible."

" Why ? "

She looked at him in astonishment. " You are a German. I am an American."

" Germans and Americans have married many times before."

" It is different now." Then she said, " Have you ever been to America ? "

" Only once—to New York for a week."

She said, not wanting to hurt or offend him, " Then you can't understand. You see, if you're to understand, we must talk honestly. You won't mind ? You won't be offended ? "

He smiled and said an odd thing, " I am not Hitler or Goebbels . . . out of the gutter."

" You must understand how different Americans are from Germans. Americans are good-natured. They're sloppy and careless. They're gamblers. They hate wars and armies and everything that goes with them. They don't like being told what to do." She looked at him again. He was smiling but he said nothing.

" You must know that it is only a matter of time until we shall be at war with you."

He interrupted her. " Oh, no. Your people won't be so foolish."

[122]

"It isn't as simple as that. They're not likely to consider whether they're being foolish or not. Besides, even if things were different and it were possible and I might consider it, it would be an insane idea for both of us."

"I do not see why. We are two intelligent people who know the world, not a pair of children. Most good marriages in Europe are made on that basis."

She thought, "How little he knows about me." There was still plenty of Annie Scanlon in her, plenty of the wild, proud young girl who had run away across the river to spend long week-ends with Tom. And there was always the curiously blurred image of Tom and Lambert in the background. She still believed in love. She had believed in it all along, all during the dreary years with Ezra Bolton, all during the years in Europe.

"Don't you see that if this war ever ends, I could never go to your country nor could you come to mine—not for years. That is the way it will be."

He did not answer her at once. Then he said, "I've never known American people very well. I've heard they were a little crazy."

Suddenly she was angry and made a great effort to control herself. "Yes," she said, "crazy like the French, like the Russians." Very nearly she said, "Germans are a little like the lunatic who believes everyone is crazy but himself." But she checked herself in time. Instead she said, "That is the way it will be. Germans won't be able to go anywhere when this is finished."

He glanced at her in astonishment, "Germans will be able to go anywhere—as conquerors."

She asked, "Do you really believe that?"

"Look at how things are now. We are winning everywhere."

She was aware that the statement was difficult to answer, yet she knew in her heart, with a curious certainty, that no matter how things looked now, the Germans would never win. Why she *knew* this she could not say, but it had to do with people like Lambert and the *Archiprêtre* and Madame Ritz and the baker's wife and the Mayor of Gerbevilliers.

She said, "I asked if you believed the Germans would be the conquerors."

For a moment he sat thinking, staring into his brandy glass. Then he said, "No." Without conviction he added, "But they will gain much."

[123]

She liked him for that. She liked him because it made him seem for a moment un-German. It raised them both to the level of intelligent individualists. Always he had puzzled her, quite outside the realm of like or dislike. Indeed, he even had a curious kind of heavy fascination.

"I think there is nothing to be gained by talking about it. I am grateful to you for everything."

He looked at her wearily, "Then you are against us too?"

"Yes . . . I think from the time your planes machine-gunned us on the road to Blois. That is something I can never understand. They accomplished so little by machine-gunning a lot of poor refugees . . . and they lost so much. It was a small thing in itself, but it has great significance. It is the kind of thing which can defeat you."

"Your side has done the same sort of thing."

The use of the words "your side" made her know that he had accepted the wall between them, and for a moment she was frightened lest she had lost all his influence. But she could not refrain from asking, "You don't believe that, do you?"

"No. It is only what I am supposed to say."

The restaurant was very nearly empty. She glanced at her watch and saw that it was nearly two o'clock. There was no one anywhere near who could hear their talk. Perhaps, she thought, that was why he had for a moment or two been wholly honest. She was aware that they had not said all they wanted to say to each other. She suspected that there was much more he wanted to say, and she asked, "Why did you ask me to marry you, when you knew it was impossible?"

Very quietly, astonishingly he said, "I was clutching at a straw." Then after a moment he added, "You are rich. You are beautiful like a work of art. I thought too that you were cold. I no longer believe that. You must have known that I admired you for a long time. I never was in love with you."

He looked down for a moment silently at his glass. "I've never been in love with any woman." Then he smiled. "It's not what you are thinking. I've had mistresses but there was no love in it. There are lots of Germans like me . . . who live and die, have mistresses, or marry and have children, without ever being in love in the way you others talk of it. I'm not even sure what you mean by 'being in love.' It is something I'm sure I have never experienced. That is one reason perhaps why we are such good servants of the state. Sometimes I think it is a kind of curse placed upon us." He fell silent and lighted a cigarette but she did not speak, for she was aware that he had not finished.

Then he said, " You see, if things had been different, a marriage between us would not have been so impossible. I have things to offer you—or had them—a fine house in Berlin, a great place in Pomerania as big as a Balkan state, a fine position . . ." His voice trailed off wearily, as if he were bored by what he was saying. Then he crushed out his cigarette and sighed, " But it is all over . . . what might have been."

She was aware that the evening was finished, that she would hear nothing more that came out of the inside of him. She said, " Do you mind if I go home ? I'm very tired."

" No. Perhaps it's best." Then he said, " I am grateful that you let me talk. I think we know each other better now . . . so well I can tell you why I really wanted to marry you . . . because I am tired and sick and corrupt and you are strong and healthy and young."

They did not walk back to the Ritz. Outside the restaurant a big grey car waited for them with a young, good-looking blond soldier at the wheel and another boy beside him with a revolver slung from one shoulder. It was clear that Von Kleist was not taking any chances of a knife in the back.

At the door of the Ritz he told the driver to wait for him and came inside. Then he said, " There is one more thing I want to tell you. Could we talk for a moment or two ? "

The corridor was empty save for the man at the concierge's desk. They sat on one of the great sofas and Von Kleist said, " There's another reason I asked you to dine. It's about the money. I can't get any more through for you or at most only a very little. The Americans are being hard about it. It isn't easy any more, even to get it through Basel. If I go away, nothing at all will come through."

She felt suddenly sick. " I must find a way. I must . . ." She thought, " I can't give it up. I can't leave all those wretched people."

" I see no way," he said abruptly. " There is nothing I can do about it. It is your own people. They are determined that we are not to have American dollars."

[125]

" What am I to do ? " she asked, almost as if speaking to herself. " What am I to do ? "

It wasn't only the poor people depending upon her for help, all the poor, dispossessed, wretched refugees, it was something else, something deeper. It would mean an end to all that she had been doing, to all the things which had brought savour and reality into her existence. And there was Lambert and the baby and Miss Godwin and no roots to return to.

Again as if speaking to herself she said, " I don't know what I'll do. I don't know."

Von Kleist was talking again, " I wanted to see you to-night to tell you to get out of all this and go back to your own country. It is really none of your business—any of this. Things are going to be ugly. They are getting worse all the time. You are very sentimental about this refugee business. They are doomed in any case, because that is the way things are."

When she did not answer him, he said, " If you are determined to stay and must have money, you could sell some of your things. You have jewellery and furs, very valuable ones."

The panic left her quickly and in its place came a sense of relief and security. It was stupid of her not to have thought of this before, but always before there had been money, more money than she could spend or find means of giving away.

She heard him saying, " I think I could find a buyer for you . . . a man of some importance who collects emeralds. And he would like his wife to have the finest sable coat in Europe. Would you consider it ? "

She tried to control the eagerness in her voice. Her quick mind told her that the prospective buyer must be a German. No one else in Europe could buy emeralds and sables. She must not seem eager, for if a German was buying these things, he must pay a good price.

" What do you think of the idea ? " the Colonel was asking.

" I think it is an excellent one. I would be grateful if you could arrange it for me."

" When are you leaving Paris ? "

" I had planned to leave to-morrow, but I will stay until the sale can be arranged."

" I will do it as quickly as possible. The buyer is an important person. Would you mind going to him ? "

" No."

" I will ring you up to-morrow." Then he stood up. " You must be very tired."

He went with her to the lift where he said, " Good-night. Good luck." And clicking his heels, kissed her hand.

She did not fall asleep for a long time because her mind was awake suddenly and would not let her sleep. Many things went through it in a strange muddled procession, the business of finding a way to carry on, Von Kleist's statement that she had better leave because things would only grow worse and worse. The whole evening had had a strange effect upon her, related somehow to that strange sensation she had experienced in the notary's house in Gerbevilliers after her talk with Harriette Godwin. It was as if she were suddenly acquiring wisdom and understanding. The conversation with Von Kleist left her confused, almost with pity for him . . . a pity which she resented and thrust from her. They had come very near to each other in a fashion which puzzled her. She wanted to help him, but there was no way for her to help. She understood now why he had wanted to marry her and the knowledge appealed to something maternal in her, and this, she knew, was dangerous because it confused all issues and left her without judgment.

The first light of morning showed through the curtains and the men outside had begun washing the streets before she fell asleep.

She slept late the next day and on waking, received a message from the concierge saying that a man was waiting downstairs with a package which must be delivered to her personally. When she asked the concierge the source of the package, he left the telephone for a moment and returned to say that it was from Cartier, the jeweller. For a moment she hesitated, puzzled, and then said, " Tell him to come up in half an hour."

She had finished her bath and done her hair and put on a dressing-gown when the knock on the door came. For a second she experienced a sensation of doubt and suspicion. No one in Paris could be sending her jewels from Cartier—at least not jewels so valuable that they must be delivered in person. The knock was repeated and curiosity overcame whatever small physical fear she experienced. Quickly she went to the door and opened it.

Outside stood Captain Jean Pierre Lambert in the cheap raincoat. He was carrying a small paper-wrapped parcel. He was smiling as he stepped past her into the room.

She closed the door quickly and said, " You shouldn't have come here."

He still smiled as he laid the parcel on the table.

" There is the parcel," he said. " There's nothing in it. It is only part of the trick."

She remembered suddenly stories she had heard, stories Von Kleist had told her, perhaps indiscreetly, of telephones which recorded conversations even when not in use.

" Be quiet," she said, and pulled out the plug of the telephone from its place beneath the table. She was trembling now, not so much from fear as from excitement at seeing him, at knowing that for some reason he had come to see her and not the baby. He still smiled at her and she was aware that somehow this meeting was different from the others. They were nearer to each other. It was almost as if in the conspiracy they were old friends. She had a curious feeling that it was so because of what had happened with Von Kleist the night before, that in some way what had happened with Von Kleist served to release something inside her.

When she turned away from the table, he said, " Did you enjoy your dinner with Von Kleist last night ? "

" Yes."

" We might have got him last night between here and Maxim's. We might have done it but for your being with him."

She did not smile back, for she experienced a sense of horror at what he was saying, that things like this had reality, that they were spoken of casually as if they were nothing at all. And suddenly, inexplicably, she did not want Von Kleist to die. That was the curious quality of the world in which she was living.

" You can't stay here long. They'll get suspicious. Why did you come ? "

" May I sit down ? "

" Naturally."

He sat down and said, " You're right. I mustn't take too long. I came to tell you that you should get out while there's time and it's not too difficult."

She thought, "That's the third time I've been warned in twenty-four hours—by Madame Ritz, by Von Kleist and now by Jean Lambert."

"I don't want to go," she said, thinking selfishly, "Where shall I go? What would I have to take the place of what I'm doing?"

"I think it's better," he said gravely. "For you and the boy both. I've changed my mind. I want you to take him with you."

Before she could answer someone knocked at the door. Jean Lambert stood up quickly and walked to the paper parcel on the table. "Open the door," he said in a low voice. "I'll be opening the parcel."

She opened the door but outside stood no one more dangerous than a porter, an old man with a drooping grey moustache. He said, "Excuse me, Madame. The telephone operator has been ringing you but the bell didn't ring. She said the call was important. May I look at the telephone?"

There was nothing to be done. "Yes," she said. "It's over there."

He crossed the room without looking at Jean Lambert who stood there occupied in untying the parcel. Quickly he discovered what the trouble was and explained.

"Odd," said Anna, "I must have kicked it out without noticing it." Then she said, "Wait!" and took out a ten-franc note from her purse and gave it to him. "Thank you," he said, and the old man went out closing the door behind him. Then she turned to Jean Lambert. "Do you think he was a real porter?"

"I don't know." Jean smiled again. "No one knows any more who anyone is." He leaned against the edge of the table and as he did so the telephone rang.

She picked it up—there was nothing else to do—and in a second she heard the voice of Von Kleist.

He told her that a rendezvous with the important personage had been arranged. It was for five that afternoon. He would call for her.

She put down the receiver and said, "That was Von Kleist. He has arranged for me to sell my sable coat and some jewellery to someone high in the Nazi government. I can get no more of my money into France."

"Make them pay well. They'll pay you in their filthy marks that are really worth nothing."

"They'll buy food and medicine here."

"That's true."

The incident of the porter still troubled her. She said, "Say what you wanted to say and go quickly." And all the time her heart was crying out, "Don't go! Don't go! Stay! Stay for ever!" He was watching her now, his head a little on one side, the mouth quite still but the eyes smiling. Like this he brought back such memories of Tom that she wanted to cry out.

"It's this," he said, "I want you to go away and take the boy with you. Give me an address that will reach you. I have no address. I live nowhere. But if I have to run for it or if this is ever finished, I can find you there."

She thought quickly. She had no address. She had no roots anywhere. The idea of her lawyer went swiftly through her mind, but he was in America. That was far away and she had a strange certainty that it would be a long time before she would be in America. Then it came to her.

"Claridge's Hotel, London. In Brook Street. I'll write it down for you."

"No," he said quickly. "It might not be good for you if they caught me and found on me an address in your hand-writing. I can remember it . . . see . . . I'll say it . . . Claridge's Hotel, Brook Street, London."

"That's it."

He picked up his hat. "I'll go now."

For a second there was a curious sense of tension as if he were uncertain what to do. They stood looking at each other, as if he meant to take her in his arms but dared not do it. She felt the colour rising in her face.

Then he took her hand and kissed it. "Good-bye," he said, "and thank you."

"I shan't go away at once," she said. "I suppose that sooner or later I shall have to go. If I am no longer in the house at Gerbevilliers you'll know where I have gone."

Then he went quickly into the hall and walked towards the servants' stairway.

When he had gone she threw the paper parcel into the waste-paper basket and went to the window where she stood for a long time looking down into the garden, smiling without knowing it.

She was thinking of many things—that it was extraordinary to find herself in the very centre of a kind of melodrama with Von Kleist on one side and Jean Pierre Lambert on the other. She was aware that hers was not the only melodrama being played in France. It was going on everywhere all about her. Melodrama had become the order of things. It had become the way of life. It was extraordinary, too, how people adjusted themselves perfectly naturally to it. The resilience of the human race was an amazing thing. Perhaps it was the reason for its long existence, that it could endure war and starvation, persecution and misery, always adjusting itself somehow.

And there was this strange business of Tom. It was more and more as if he had come back. Jean Pierre Lambert reminded her of Tom in the quality of his voice, the way he held a cigarette between thumb and forefinger, the way he walked, all his mannerisms. There was something frightening about it. For a moment when he looked at her with his head a little on one side, smiling, she had almost cried out, " Tom ! Tom ! "

Strange speculations filled her head of things unknown and unknowable. For a long time after Tom's death she had experienced moments when he seemed very near to her, in the same room, as if he had returned to speak to her. Afterwards when the moments grew more rare and finally ceased to occur, she dismissed the experience as hysteria and unreasonable. In any case, there had been no place in the life of a brisk, hardworking secretary for such nonsense. But now the memory of the sensation returned, vividly, as if Tom had come back again.

" That is all nonsense," she thought, " I must not think of it."

But most of all, as she stood there by the window looking down into the garden, she knew that she was happy again for the first time since Tom had died. She knew that Jean Lambert now trusted her so much that he was willing to leave his son to her. And she knew, too, that there was an understanding between them of which neither of them had betrayed a sign. But most of all, he respected her. The feeling of indignity and shame that came over her when he slapped her face in the darkness crying out, " I know your kind. You are the cause of everything," was gone.

The ringing of the telephone roused her. In a kind of trance she crossed the room and picked it up. The voice was that of Madame Ritz. She said that she was kept in her room, in bed, by orders of the doctor. The night before she had had a heart attack. It was very tiresome being shut in—would Anna drop in later about tea time and talk for a while.

You must understand that when Anna told me all this she was a quite different Anna from the one who cut me at the top of the stairs in Haddonfield House. That is really what this story is about—how Anna changed and came to be born at last as a whole person, without deformity, how Anna learned understanding and humanity and the value of things in life. If she had not changed, she could never have told me all the story—how she felt about Von Kleist and what had happened to her in the room when Lambert left after delivering the bogus package.

You must never think that she was not intelligent, or that she did not have a certain objectivity about what was happening to her. A stupid woman would never have understood it, step by step, even while it was happening. A stupid woman could never have used Von Kleist nor have held his friendship in spite of everything. A stupid woman would never have become involved in the whole tangle of events which so changed her life. Anna's whole story is that of an extremely intelligent and clever woman whose whole life was deformed by the circumstances of her childhood and early youth. But she was an emotional woman, too, with a tremendous capacity for love and affection which, like so much else in her existence, was for a long time baffled and frustrated. That was what Miss Godwin knew well. That was what held people like Miss Godwin and myself loyal to Anna through everything. That warmth was always there, however concealed and deformed. You could not know Anna without understanding this.

Only a clever woman would have suspected what was happening to her. Only an intelligent woman would have understood it while it was happening. It was a little, too, that she was growing up at last, learning that peculiar sort of wisdom which only comes through living, and from the pain growing out of the entanglement of one life with another.

Afterwards she said, " I began to understand that. I began to understand that Von Kleist was so strange, so frustrated because his life had always been apart from the lives of others.

Nothing had ever really happened to him which he had not sought and planned for in cold blood—and those things bring no wisdom and no more than a superficial satisfaction because they are contrived and in themselves superficial. That is what makes people who have always been materially successful sometimes so dull and so shallow."

Von Kleist called for her in a big grey car and they drove to a house in the Rue de la Faisanderie near the Bois, an immense house with a big courtyard for parking cars on the occasion of dinners and balls. At sight of it, Anna experienced a vague sense of recognition, of having been there before, but it was not until she walked into the big hall that she recognized it by the tapestries, the over-lush furnishing, the great marble stairway. It had belonged in the old days to Oppenheimer, a Dutch Jew who had made a vast fortune out of manipulating foreign exchange between the two wars. When she had dined there last he had been one of the richest men in Europe. Since then he had simply disappeared, no one knew where, another of the casualties in a world which no longer existed.

At the door, in the big hallway, everywhere, there were guards. As they entered, a young adjutant came towards them saluting, and when Von Kleist explained his mission, the adjutant disappeared. While they waited Anna regarded the opulence of the establishment. "Kings," she thought, "no longer live like this . . . with all this luxury and a guard at every door." The personage they had come to see must be someone very great indeed. Still Von Kleist gave no hint of his identity.

She began thinking over what she meant to say. At first she had considered taking Monsieur de Jong from Cartier and Monsieur Le Blanc from Revillon with her, to do the bargaining, but this idea she had dismissed at once both as impossible and unnecessary. She had seen them both earlier in the afternoon and they had suggested the prices she should ask for the emeralds and the sable coat. They had even suggested allowing them to do all the bargaining, but this idea too she had rejected. The great personage might bully them as a German could bully a tradesman with a fortune at stake in occupied Paris. Her, as an American, he could not bully. Monsieur de Jong had said, "You can get a good price. If he is a big enough personage in the Nazi scheme of things, price will not matter. Those at the top just take the

[133]

money they need." Now, as she sat waiting, she was a little excited by the prospect of bargaining.

Then the young adjutant reappeared and led them up the huge marble stairway. A little way along the hall he opened a door and said in a loud voice, " Herr Colonel Baron Eric Von Kleist und Frau Bolton."

As she walked through the door she recognized the great personage at once. At sight of her he lifted his immense soft bulk with difficulty from a sofa and came towards her grinning. It was the grin of a sick, unnatural person. It made her feel a little ill. He was dressed in a pale blue uniform that stretched too tightly about the bulges of fat, outlining too obviously the vast buttocks and the great, almost feminine breasts hung with medals. The eyes were pale blue and small with great bags beneath them. The round head was covered with thinning hair that gave the impression of having been dyed pale blond. It was a monster who came towards her, the too-small petulant mouth relaxed in a smile. There was no mistaking him. It was the great Field Marshal himself.

A little behind him stood a great blonde Brunhild of a woman. Von Kleist presented Anna and she felt suddenly that the great bloated mass half-expected a curtsy which she did not give him. She experienced a sudden, swift, purely female sense of disgust and revulsion. The woman whom Von Kleist introduced as the Field Marshal's wife seemed pleasant enough and handsome in a Wagnerian fashion.

The conversation was stiff and awkward, conducted in a strange mixture of French, German and English. It appeared that the Field Marshal and his wife knew a great deal about her and what she was doing. He complimented her on her work, and expressed a slight wonder over Americans who were always doing things for other people without any prospect of reward or gain. He had a curious voice, rather small and soft and flute-like, a tiny voice to come out of such a mountain of flesh.

An orderly, who had obviously once been a butler, with two other soldiers, brought in tea and sherry and cakes.

The room was a handsome room with a Louis Quinze *boiserie* of natural wood partly gilded. All the furniture, the *bibelots*, were magnificent. It was just as Oppenheimer had left it. Anna thought, " When things begin to go wrong, they will strip the place and take everything to Berlin."

The room, the gestures of tea and sherry, the stilted talk should have been civilized but were not. Over it all lay a curious coating of barbarism, of imitation, of awkwardness which was very German. The Field Marshal and even his big, handsome wife were grotesque against the civilized luxurious background. Even Von Kleist himself seemed stiff and ungracious and out of place.

Anna felt both uncomfortable and hostile and as she sat there, minute by minute, an hysterical desire to rise from her chair and run from the room kept growing. Never had she experienced more acutely the sense of " strangeness " which set most Germans apart from other people. But it was more than that. As she sat there making stiff conversation, she knew that sooner or later—perhaps very soon—whatever she was doing would come to an end, that Madame Ritz and Von Kleist and Jean Pierre were right. Everything would grow worse and worse. It was not possible for the world to submit to men like this monster sitting opposite her now, his fat buttocks pressed between the arms of a fragile Louis Quinze chair. It was not possible even for the rest of the world to deal with such men. It would be a bitter fight, to the end, to death and extermination for one side or the other.

The bargaining for the coat came quickly. It appeared that the Field Marshal felt no need to see the coat or the emeralds. His furrier had told him that it was the finest sable coat in Europe and that the emeralds were famous, especially one ring which he wanted for himself. When he talked of the emeralds, a look of covetousness, almost of impotent desire, came into the pale, piggish blue eyes. Then it was for the first time that she noticed the make-up on the fat face, applied very skilfully even to shadows under the eyes in order to conceal the effect of the pouches. " This," she thought, " is one of the leaders of the German people. Another is a paranoiac called Hitler, a third a little club-footed sex maniac, another a sadist . . ."

Disgust and hatred again took possession of her.

But she stuck to her price, taking satisfaction in gaining her end. The Field Marshal at first showed an inclination to haggle, but she said simply, " You understand. I am not personally in need of money. I am an immensely rich woman. It is only that it has become more and more difficult to get money into France for my work. The emeralds and the sables mean nothing to me.

I have finished with all that. What I am interested in is the money I can get for them—the best price possible, not for myself but for what I can do with the money."

After that speech the Field Marshal stopped haggling, as if he were ashamed. Like Von Kleist, he said, "I do not see why you care so much for these pigs of refugees. It would be better if they died. They will die in any case. You merely prolong their unfortunate existence."

She did not answer him, but forced through the deal as quickly as possible. She was to be paid the equivalent of thirty thousand dollars in Reichsmarks for the sables and the equivalent of one hundred and twenty thousand for the emeralds, all in cash. That was a tremendous amount of money. It would buy a vast amount of food and medical supplies.

The Field Marshal rose with difficulty from his chair and she knew that it was a sign for her to leave.

As she went out of the door, Von Kleist lingered for a moment to talk to the Field Marshal. In the hall she waited for him, watched all the time by the two soldiers who stood just outside.

All the way back to the Ritz, Von Kleist sat beside her, brooding and depressed. It was as if he were ashamed of what she had seen, as if he was enough of an international to understand the revulsion of feeling she experienced.

In the bar they had a cocktail among all the noisy officers and their women and for a long time he remained silent. At last he said, "I have got what I wanted. I am going to Russia to-morrow."

Politely she said, "I'm glad you got what you wanted. I don't imagine I shall stay much longer in France. Perhaps we shall meet after the war." What she said was merely a conventional speech. She had no desire any longer ever to see him again.

He ordered another cocktail and sat staring at it moodily and presently he said, "I doubt that we shall meet. What happens to me is of no importance. In trying to gain the whole world we have lost it for ever. God help the German people for generations to come."

She did not answer him but stood up and said, "I must go now. I'm going to talk with Madame Ritz before dinner. You need not go with me. Stay and finish your drink."

He rose and kissed her hand and walked to the door of the bar with her. Then he looked at her for a moment and said, "Good-bye and good luck. If things had been different . . ."

"But they aren't," she said, and left him. She never saw him again.

In her room she took up the telephone and called Madame Ritz's apartment. A strange woman's voice answered, and when Anna asked, "May I speak to Madame Ritz—this is Mrs. Bolton?" the voice answered, "Madame Ritz cannot speak over the telephone." And then after a second, "Monsieur Beck will explain to you. Can you receive him now?"

"Yes. At any time."

She put down the telephone, filled with an unaccountable sense of weariness and depression. She took off her hat and ran a comb through her hair. Seeing herself in the glass she thought, "Where are you going? What is to happen to you? You are thirty-eight years old and still you belong nowhere, to nothing, to nobody!"

Then there was a knock at the door and old Monsieur Beck, the manager, stood there. He was an old, heavy man, rather clumsily built, with white hair and a white moustache. He was of the little band which had begun long ago with César and Marie Ritz to build a great tradition. He was one of the last of them.

Now, in his soft voice, he said, "I am sorry to disturb you. I came to explain why Madame Ritz could not speak to you. She died a little while ago, very quietly."

The old man turned away to hide the tears he could not control.

She thanked him and he went quickly away, and when he had gone she sat for a long time in the fading twilight, relaxed and a little dazed, scarcely thinking at all. She was only aware of a sense of complete and final disintegration of the world about her. It was all over!

The business with the Field Marshal was finished the next day, and without waiting for the funeral of Madame Ritz she returned to Gerbevilliers. Before she left she went through her trunks in the storeroom of the Ritz, taking with her as many of the things as she could manage to pack into two bags she found there. It was a depressing business, going through trunks filled with gowns and books and *bibelots* that she had left behind. Looking at them now they seemed to belong not to a life which had finished only a little while ago but a life as remote as that of Lewisburg and the

Flats. Seeing all these remnants of the past, touching them again, seeing again all the people and scenes which they brought to mind, filled her with a sense of mingled sadness and relief. It was like going through the trunk left for generations in the attic of an old house.

There were surprisingly few things she wanted to take with her. All the things which once had seemed so important now had no use or importance at all. They gave her a sense of utter futility, of something which was finished for ever.

When she left the storeroom she called Rose, the chambermaid, whom she had known for years and told her, " You may have everything I have left there. I shan't want them. Very likely you can sell them."

She had a curious feeling of clairvoyance that from now on she would be travelling light, perhaps for the rest of her life. The gesture filled her with a sense of satisfaction, as if she had cut loose clearly from everything and was in a way reborn. From the moment she closed the lid of the last trunk, she began to be aware of a feeling of change in her destiny. Again it was closely akin to the feeling of freedom which had come to her on the night in the notary's house when the barriers between her and Miss Godwin were broken down for ever.

Now she wanted to hurry back to Gerbevilliers. She wanted to leave this strange grey Paris filled with Germans and traitors —the Paris she had once loved more than any city she had ever known. Beside it the ugly little notary's house seemed cosy and pleasant. Paris was a dead city now, filled with ghosts.

From the window of the dirty, crowded train she watched the city slipping away from her, perhaps for ever. Now that Von Kleist had gone off to the steppes of Russia, the chances of wangling papers and privileges seemed very slight indeed, for it was no longer any good getting favours through the traitors she had known in the old life. They hadn't much power any more. Some had fled the country. Some were dead. Those who remained had little power or influence and were paralysed by fear. One had to go to the Germans for everything.

The train reached Gerbevilliers at dusk. She was glad to arrive, to escape the people sitting opposite her, who looked a little starved, in whom all spirit was dead. Following a long-established custom, she left her luggage at the station to be brought on later by André, son of the *Chef de Gare*, in a hand-cart.

Carrying only a small bag, she set out to walk to the house of the notary.

It was a misty night in November, cold, with a new moon shining above the mist. She was very tired from the long uncomfortable journey and the walk through the crisp air made her feel better. Her brain began to work again, clearly and practically. Now that she was away from Paris, with its curious atmosphere of paralysis and death and confusion, she saw what she must do. She must plan for the wife of the Mayor to take over the brickyard. Madame Herbet was a good woman even though a little disorganized. But Madame St. Genis, the baker's wife, could help her. She had the qualities Madame Herbet lacked. In any case there was nobody else in Gerbevilliers to whom she could entrust the work.

If the worst came to the worst there were the hundreds of thousands of Reichsmarks in the bag she carried. They would go a long way if anyone could find anything to buy with them. She herself would stay on as long as possible.

Now thinking over all that had happened in Paris, all the warnings she had received, it was clear that no one believed that her being an American citizen would protect her any longer. It was only a question of time until she too would become an enemy alien to the Germans. Staying behind to be shut up in a concentration camp would serve no purpose. It would only be foolish. As she walked she came to a decision. To-morrow she must see the wife of the Mayor and make arrangements for her to carry on.

The streets through which she walked were silent and empty and the houses dark. Most citizens of Gerbevilliers were in bed by now, because there was no light and very little heat. She liked the sense of being alone. There was something clean and refreshing about it. It gave her a sense of being strong and indefatigable.

"I suppose," she thought, "that is because I have always been alone. Ever since Tom died—until that night when Harriette and I understood each other."

She would be a lone wolf now, on her own, trusting her own health and strength and wits alone, but for Miss Godwin. The idea of Miss Godwin still troubled her. Miss Godwin ought to be safe in New York in a comfortable flat, and not here in a dying provincial town, cold and without proper food. If it

[139]

became necessary to run for it, to get to the border with or without papers, Miss Godwin would be a great handicap. Very likely she would die before she ever reached safety.

She crossed the empty unlighted square and turned into her own street. Somewhere a dog was baying at the moon, making a queer mournful sound which set her imagination to work. She thought, " This is how the world will be when all the men on it have killed each other off . . . a dark and empty town with only a dog howling at the moon."

A little way up the street she saw the faint light filtering out between the closed shutters on the house of the notary, and a feeling of warmth came over her. This was home—as much of a home as she had ever known since Tom died. Harriette Godwin would be there, seated by the little iron stove, working by the light of a kerosene lamp, and the baby would be already asleep in his crib.

He was getting to be a big boy. He could walk a few steps and make sounds which were beginning to take form. He called her " *Tante*." Suddenly she knew how much this strange child meant to her, that she could not face the idea of being separated from him, that nothing must happen to him. He was her own, as much as if he were a part of her flesh. It was all tied up with the strange business of Tom and Jean Pierre Lambert and her own dead baby. She knew that well enough but she did not push the idea lest she bruise or destroy the illusion which she had come earnestly to cherish. Perhaps it was wrong to feel as happy as she felt now. Perhaps something terrible would happen. . . .

The door was locked, which seemed odd, since neither she nor Miss Godwin ever troubled to lock it. Sudden fears seized her and she pulled the handle of the old-fashioned bell so violently that even in the street she could hear its tinny jangle in the distant kitchen. After a moment the sound of heavy footsteps sounded on the tiles of the little hallway. It was not Miss Godwin who was answering the clamour of the bell; Miss Godwin walked lightly like a bird.

Then the door opened and with a wild sensation of relief she recognized the fat figure of Marguerite, the cook.

" Good evening, Madame," she said.

Anna stepped inside and closed the door. " Is anything wrong, Marguerite ? " she asked.

"The old Mademoiselle is ill. Doctor Chastel said she must stay in bed, so I've been spending the nights here."

In the little *salon* Anna took off her coat and hat. "And the baby?" she asked.

Marguerite smiled, "The baby is fine. He can say ' *Tante* ' now quite clearly. I have been teaching him."

"What is it Mademoiselle has?"

"Doctor Chastel says it is influenza. She came in soaking wet from the brickyard two days ago. I scolded her but it was too late to do any good. She already had influenza."

"What does the Doctor say about it?"

"He says it will be all right if it doesn't turn into pneumonia."

Anna was thoughtful for a moment. "Is she awake?"

"I don't know. She has a high fever. She sleeps and wakes in turns. Not for very long. Would Madame like something to eat?"

She was hungry. Her health was good and her appetite keen. "Yes. You might open a tin of soup and make some tea. Is there bread?"

"Yes, Madame. Somehow the baker has got flour again."

"I'll go and see her now."

But before she went to Miss Godwin she picked up the lamp and went into her bedroom to have a look at the baby. He was lying on his back with both arms over his head. The sight of him produced a strange excitement in her and brought the image of his father again into her mind. He was a handsome baby with his dark curls and high colour, and very sturdy.

Reluctantly she left him and, still carrying the lamp, she went into the passage and up the stairs to Miss Godwin's room. As she opened the door softly, Miss Godwin turned her head to look at her.

"Oh," she said, "I *am* glad you're back."

"I stayed longer than I expected. There was trouble about the money. It gets more difficult each time."

"Did you get it?" Miss Godwin asked anxiously.

"Yes, all I needed."

She would not tell Harriette now what had happened or how she got the money. Perhaps she would never tell her.

"How are you feeling?" she asked.

"A little better, I think."

She seemed bright enough but there was a curious note of weariness in her voice that had never been there before.

Anna sat down by the bed and took her hand. It was very hot, but what shocked her was its thinness. The dry hot skin was stretched over the bones. She was ashamed of not having noticed this before.

" Would you like some broth ? "

" No, thanks. Marguerite brought me some a little while ago. She's been very good—Marguerite—leaving her husband and children to look after themselves."

Anna almost said, " When we go away I'm giving her a present of a handful of Reichsmarks. They'll help with the children." And then checked herself. It would be no good worrying Miss Godwin now with the news that sooner or later they must leave.

" How did things go in Paris ? "

" Very well—on the whole."

" Did you see Madame Ritz ? "

" Yes."

" How is she ? "

" Tired."

" She is in a difficult position. She is a very remarkable woman." Miss Godwin coughed and then said, " You must be very tired, Anna. I'm quite all right. I'll go to sleep presently. Get some rest. You'll have double work with me laid up like this. Go along, now ! "

Anna rose and bent down as if to kiss the old woman, but Miss Godwin pushed her away weakly, " No, my dear. Don't do that ! We can't both be ill. You shouldn't even have come into the room."

Anna laughed, " It doesn't matter. I'm as strong as an ox. I never catch anything. Good-night, my dear."

" Good-night, Anna."

She went out leaving Miss Godwin. As she descended the stairs she knew that Miss Godwin was going to die, that, somehow, she was willing to die. She did not know for certain how old she was. She had never asked her her age.

Before getting into bed, Anna stood again for a moment over the crib of the baby. What lay before him ? What kind of life would he have ? What kind of world would he live in ?

Upstairs in the darkness lay Harriette Godwin. What was she thinking about now ? She had lived through so many worlds. Was she thinking now about that Europe of

Edward VII, rich and comfortable and charged with menace. Or the evil reign of the robber barons in America? Or of the world which had collapsed, leaving her penniless as an old woman. Or the mad, doomed carnival dispersed at last by the war.

Little Jean Pierre stood at the beginning of a confused and shattered world, Harriette Godwin at the end of one. She was tired and ready to die.

After she was in bed, Anna lay for a long time, sleepless, her mind wandering this way and that. It was a curious experience. It was as if she were growing, as if she had been growing for a long time. The process was very painful, full of bewilderment and self-reproach.

Doctor Chastel was a very old man and the only doctor left in Gerbevilliers. He was a good man but not a very good doctor, and his ideas were very old-fashioned. He believed in giving great quantities and varieties of pills. And so he treated poor Miss Godwin. On the second morning after Anna's return he took her aside when they had descended the stairs and said gravely, "It is not good. The influenza has turned into pneumonia. We cannot do very much but hope the medicine will work."

He went away then, and a little later, after Miss Godwin had slept a little, Anna went up and sat by the bed, holding her friend's hand. For a long time Miss Godwin lay with her eyes closed, in silence, but presently she opened her eyes, turned her head and smiled at her.

"There is something I want to tell you. I want you to know it in case anything happens to me. I want you to know how grateful I am to you for all you have done for me and for all the others up there on the hill. I want you to know that I've been very happy here this last year, happier than I have ever been before in all my life."

Anna didn't say anything. She only pressed the thin hand in silence.

Miss Godwin was having difficulty in breathing. When she had recovered a little, she said, "There is something else."

Anna interrupted her. "Don't try to talk. It's bad for you."

But the old woman would not be silenced. "No," she

[143]

said, "it is something I must say. It's this. I feel I know you very well, my dear, perhaps better than I have ever known anyone." She coughed and after a moment continued, "I've seen something happen to you, my dear, something miraculous." She smiled weakly. "I think I've seen you grow a soul."

Anna turned away for a moment, pretending to occupy herself with the medicines and glasses on the little table beside the bed. When she turned back Miss Godwin's eyes were closed and she seemed to be asleep despite the difficulty of breathing. Quietly Anna lifted the thin hand and placed it on her breast. Then she went out of the room leaving the door open. It was time for her to go to the brickyard. No one had visited the prisoners for nearly four days. They must not think they were forgotten. And there was the business to settle with the Mayor's wife about the money and carrying on the work.

It was nearly seven o'clock when she returned, the visit to the camp made and arrangements completed with the Mayor's wife. Marguerite, sobbing, met her at the door to tell her that Miss Godwin was dead. She had died quietly in her sleep, quickly, without struggling to live.

Miss Harriette Godwin, born on Murray Hill, was buried in the tiny Protestant graveyard of Gerbevilliers. The service was read by Anna herself in English out of Miss Godwin's own prayerbook, since there was no Protestant pastor in the town and no way of fetching one from Lyons. The Mayor and his wife, and the *Archiprêtre* and half the town attended the service. The *Archiprêtre* said a prayer over the grave. There were few flowers at that season and none at all in either of the two little flower shops in the village, but some of the people made wreaths of evergreen and brought them to cover the bare earth of the naked grave.

In the brickyard, when Anna brought the news of Miss Godwin's death, it spread from lip to lip like flame working through the place. Sallow, weary, half-starved faces surrounded Anna whispering, muttering, crying. It was a spectacle out of Hell, with despair and death written on most of the faces. They were dying now, rapidly, sometimes as many as one or two a day, as if they no longer had the will to resist death. In one month there were three suicides. Lately rumours that the Germans were to take over all France had created fresh despair.

Surrounded by the haunted faces Anna told them that she meant to stay, that Miss Godwin's death had made no difference. If she was forced to go, or was herself interned, she had, she told them, made arrangements with others to carry on the work and had left money for it. She did not say that even money was not of much use any longer because there was little soap or chocolate or tea or medicine to be had at any price.

When she left them one old man pushed forward and kissed her hand. The gesture filled her with a wild desire to burst into tears. She managed to control herself until she had passed through the office of the Commandant, but once outside she began to weep hysterically. All the way down the barren, windswept road to the town the tears poured down her cheeks. By the time she reached the town itself, she was able to control herself, but those tears had washed away for ever whatever there remained of ego or selfishment or pride or resentment.

At home in the notary's house she wrote a letter to a cousin of Miss Godwin, an old woman who lived in South Orange, New Jersey. She was the only relative Miss Godwin had ever spoken of, the only one whose address was found among the things she left behind. Because there was not much time left she went the next day to order a gravestone for Miss Godwin's grave. The lettering was simple. It bore her name, the dates of her birth and death, and a simple inscription in English— " A good and honourable woman."

As if even Nature meant to be malicious, winter came on early, chilling the houses, the marsh and the forest, and covering them with a mantle of fog. On 1st December snow fell—thick, sticky snow that melted as soon as it touched the earth. There was no more coal—all coal was needed in Germany—and so the little iron *salamandre* stove which had served so valiantly was no longer of any use. The little fireplace, which had been sealed and covered by wallpaper, was opened up, and Anna began burning wood which old François the *charbonier* brought her from the forest. The little fireplace smoked and puffed until the fire was really under way, and even when it was burning brilliantly it did not heat the room as the fierce little stove had done.

Up at the brickyard the winter misery set in. There was not enough heat and the roof leaked so that rain and melting snow dripped through into the living quarters. Influenza swept through the place, carrying off eleven refugees who made no effort to live.

And for Anna herself there were new difficulties. When she sent her permit to travel to Paris to be renewed, it was not returned. Twice she sent letters by way of men from Lyons who were crossing the border but no answer came back. The supplies, even those stored in bulk in the garage of the Mayor, began to run out, first the soap, then the chocolate, then the iodine. But worst of all the tinned milk was giving out, the milk she needed for the baby. There remained only a case and a few extra tins with no prospect of getting more.

At times in the night, when she could not sleep, a kind of terror seized her, like that of an animal trapped in a jungle and surrounded by beaters who kept closing in, nearer and nearer. The sadness of life in Gerbevilliers began to have its effect even upon her own healthy body and temperament—no one in Gerbevilliers even laughed any more. The children grew a little thinner and more listless each day. Even the winter landscape, grey and shrouded in fog, seemed sad and defeated.

And added to the depression was the worry because she had heard nothing from Jean Lambert. She thought of him a great deal, sometimes sitting for a long time before the little fireplace, simply staring into the fire, trying to imagine where he was and what he was doing. In a strange way Tom was fading from her memory, or perhaps it was only that he had come to be identified so completely with Jean Lambert that there were no longer two men, individuals, but only one. The silence troubled her, but underneath the worry there was a curious, staunch faith that nothing would ever happen to him, that he would find her again somehow because it was meant to be like that.

In order to harden herself, she tried to tell herself that it was foolish to hope, that it was insane to allow him to make so much difference to her, that surely one day or another he would be captured or killed. But she did not really believe any of these things. She was always sure in the depths of her heart that he would return.

It was like a story that was not finished. He had to return in order that they might carry out together a destiny designed for them. The memory of that moment in the Ritz when, just before he left, they stood looking at each other, understanding that something had happened between them, was still very strong in her memory. She returned to it again and again, sometimes in walking up the long hill to the windswept brickyard, sometimes while she sat trying to read the worn old novels out of the library of the *Archiprêtre*, sometimes in the night when she wakened and lay there, frightened, trying to push from her the awful sense of things closing in upon her. She clung to the memory of that moment as something infinitely precious. Most of all she knew that when they met again it would be different, because in that curious moment they had understood each other. They would meet as old friends, perhaps as more than that.

The baby was tied up in the whole thing. He walked quite well now and was able to say, " *Bon jour* " and " *soupe* " and to call her " *Tante* " very clearly. He had about reached the age at which her own baby had died long ago. More and more she forgot the memory of her own child and lost herself in little Jean Pierre. More and more her child and Tom's, dead long ago, *became* this child born of the refugee girl who died on the bloody road outside Villiers.

Then one morning as she passed the house of Madame St. Genis, on her way to the brickyard, the big woman came to the door and called her.

" I've been waiting for you to pass," she said ; " I have a letter for you. It was left by a man on a motor-cycle who came through here last night."

She knew at once that the message had something to do with Jean Lambert since it was delivered to Monsieur St. Genis who was " one of us." She began to tremble and her knees to shake. For a moment as she stepped inside the house she felt that she was going to faint.

From behind a canister on the shelves, Madame St. Genis took the letter and handed it to her.

Quickly she tore it open the envelope and looked for the signature. There it was—*JEAN*. He was not dead. Then at the very beginning of the letter she noticed another thing which made her heart leap. He addressed her as *Chère Amie*, not as *Madame* or even *Chère Madame*, but as *Chère Amie*, as a man addressed a woman he loved. For such things have great importance with the French for whom each form of address expresses the exact degree of intimacy. He had chosen to address her as *Chère Amie*. She had not been wrong ; she had not deceived herself about that curious moment when, without speaking, they had understood each other.

The letter was written on cheap, lined paper of the sort one found in a village *librairie*. It was very short. It read merely : " *I am writing to you to ask that you prepare yourself for a journey and be ready to leave at any time. I will have all arrangements made. There is work to be done elsewhere and it is time that you and the boy are on your way. I will come for you myself. I am sorry to hear that Miss Godwin is dead. It makes it harder for you. My sincere sympathy. I hope the boy is well and not causing you too much worry. Best wishes.—JEAN.*"

The substance of the letter meant very little to her. Already she was resigned in her heart to going away. What moved her was that he had signed the letter simply " JEAN," as if, almost shyly, he sought to establish the new relationship between them.

She was aware that the bright small eyes of Madame St. Genis were watching her, hungry with curiosity. She turned to the baker's wife and said, " It is good news. He is coming here."

" When ? " asked Madame St. Genis.

" He doesn't say when."

" He is a nice boy—a brave boy," said Madame St. Genis. " My husband is very fond of him."

All the way up the chill, windswept hill her heart sang as it had not sung since those days when she had been with Tom in the mountains of West Virginia. It was like being a young girl again, as if all the triviality, the bitterness, the tragedy which had happened in between were swept away. It was better even than that because now there was no bitterness in her heart and no resentment. For now Lewisburg and the Flats and Centre Avenue were dead for ever.

It was dark when at last she left the wretched population of the brickyard and set out for home. The bell in the church of St. Étienne was ringing, slowly and mournfully, calling worshippers to the Sunday evening Mass. There was no moon, and beneath the low-hanging mist the darkness was thick and damp and cold, almost a tangible cold as if it were possible to cut it into cubes like blocks of ice. She had to walk carefully and not too rapidly, feeling her way across streets and between the plane trees that bordered the square. It would have been difficult to

[148]

find the notary's house but for the dim light coming through the shutters. Inside the house the happiness still remained. About her heart there was a physical sensation of warmth which had been there all day, surviving even the misery she had seen at the brickyard. It was like an inner fire, belonging to her alone, unknown to everyone, even old Madame St. Genis who had seen her face when she opened the letter.

As she stepped into the *salon* she discovered the stout, short, figure of Madame St. Genis herself coming towards her. It was clear that something tremendous had happened for there was in the old woman's face and eyes an extraordinary excitement mingled with joy. For more than a year she had never seen such a look in the face of anyone. It was as if such things had gone out of the world.

Then Madame St. Genis said, "Have you heard what has happened? Japan has attacked your country. Now you will join us and we shall be free again."

Then quickly, breathlessly, Madame St. Genis told the story of the treachery of Pearl Harbour.

"We were listening to the short wave in the cellar," she said, "when suddenly the broadcast from England was broken and they told the news. It is evil. It is *infect* what they did, but it is good too, for now we shall win. Now we shall be free again."

Then the old woman began to cry hysterically and fell into a chair, covering her face with her handkerchief and rocking from side to side. It denoted monumental joy and grief, as if for too long the old woman had held herself tightly in check. For over a year there had been no future save the eternal prospect of submission and misery. And now there was hope.

Anna brought her a glass of wine and presently she stopped crying and said, "I came straight here to tell you. I'm sorry for you and your people. War is a terrible thing. But the world has changed. Now we are all in this together."

Then as she grew more calm she said, what all the others had said, "Now you must go. You must not end up like the poor people in the brickyard. You must go away quickly."

"Yes," said Anna, "now I must go."

She looked at the fat old woman. She wanted suddenly to weep because she knew suddenly how valiant a person old Madame St. Genis really was, how valiant were all the people

[149]

of the little town—the Mayor and the Mayor's wife and all the others who had helped her when she came there as a stranger. They were old friends now—and comrades. Miss Godwin lay in the graveyard by the clear little river. She herself had roots in this place, the first real roots she had ever known. Whatever happened she would come back to Gerbevilliers, in better times when there would be money again, when she could use money. Now, to-night, everything was black, save for the knowledge that she loved old, fat Madame St. Genis and the Mayor and the Mayor's wife and the little people of the town and the wretched ones in the brickyard on the windswept hill above the town. She knew what it was to love her fellow-people. Suddenly it seemed to her that she had been born here, in the little provincial town of Gerbevilliers, and had never had any other life.

But Madame St. Genis was putting on her coat and saying that she had to be back because her husband would be wanting to go to bed. He couldn't go to sleep without her in bed beside him.

At the door Anna suddenly put her arms about Madame St. Genis, embracing her French fashion, and suddenly both of them were in tears again.

But there was work to be done.

The next day she put her accounts in order and took the books over to the Mayor's wife along with the rest of the money, all save a little she would need for the journey to . . . She did not know where Jean meant to take her—perhaps to Spain, perhaps to Switzerland, perhaps to Africa. There was mystery and a sense of adventure about it and a curious sense of satisfaction in having the decision made for her by a man with whom she was in love. She was aware of how long she had been alone, of how long she had had to live making her own decisions, being the strong one upon whom all others leaned. She knew suddenly that she was very tired, that she wanted desperately to be cared for and protected.

At home in the notary's house she waited night after night, two small bags packed, one with the baby's things and one with her own, ready to leave. Each evening Madame St. Genis came in with the news she had gleaned from the British broadcast heard over the radio in the cellar. The net drew closer and closer. Germany and Italy declared war on the United States and overnight Anna became an enemy alien. It only remained now for the Germans to take over the rest of France and make her a prisoner like the people in the brickyard on the hill. When night after night passed without any word from Jean, she began to be terrified lest he had forgotten her or had been captured or killed.

And then one night a little after dark there was a knock at the door and it happened as she imagined so many times it would happen. When she opened the door he was standing there, not this time in a cheap suit and raincoat but dressed in a steel-grey uniform, looking very neat and handsome. Behind him, at the kerb, she saw a kind of half-ruined delivery van.

He said, " I've come for you. Are you ready ? "

" Yes. It will only take a moment."

He followed her into the little *salon* and then into the bedroom where he stood watching while she took the nightgown made by Miss Godwin off the baby and dressed him. He was very good. He did not mind being wakened. It was almost as if he understood they were going on an adventure.

When he was dressed and ready, she put on the hat and coat she had chosen for the escape. They came from the local bazaar and they were cheap and dowdy, like the clothes any middle-class Frenchwoman would wear in these times. She saw him smile as he looked at her.

Then he said, " I have the papers. They are all in order. They come from Vichy." He smiled again, " We have friends even there, working inside the government. We shouldn't have any trouble."

" What is the uniform ? "

He laughed. " I am dressed as an organizer of the Youth Movement, sponsored by the Marshal. It describes me thus in the papers. I think no one will question us."

Then, still laughing, he said, " We are described as Monsieur and Madame Henri St. Genis. I hope you don't mind."

Her heart began to beat rapidly. She tried to control her voice. She managed to say, " No, of course not. Why should I mind ? "

The grin grew a little broader. " I like it," he said.

Then she picked up the baby and before turning out the kerosene lamp she looked round the ugly little room and a lump came into her throat at the thought of leaving it. " Some day," she thought, "I will come back and buy the house and come here to stay a part of every year."

Then quickly she put out the light and for a second she had a strange vivid feeling that Miss Godwin was standing there in the darkness beside her, wishing her good luck on the journey.

Out of the darkness came Jean's voice, "We'd better not waste time. We have to drive to the main line." And she felt his hand on her arm as if to guide her towards the door. And then quickly he kissed her.

It all happened swiftly in darkness and in silence. She was aware of the clean scent of tobacco, and of eau-de-Cologne, the same scent which long ago she had come to identify for ever with Tom. It was an extraordinary moment, confused and yet blinding in its clarity, a moment out of the unknown and the unknowable.

Outside he helped her to the seat beside a thin man whom he introduced only as Jacques. Then he climbed into the back of the ramshackle lorry and they drove away through the darkness along the little river out of Gerbevilliers where so little had happened and yet so much.

When Anna Bolton left Paris after selling the sables and the emeralds, she disappeared from the world. In London no one any longer even heard rumours of her. Now and then among those who still sometimes thought of what the world had been before the war, one heard people still speculate concerning what had become of Anna Bolton, remarking that it was curious that even the State Department had no information concerning her whereabouts or her fate. Now and then it was said that she had died or that she was in a concentration camp. But no one really knew anything at all.

With the great blitz finished and London settled back into a relieved sense of security, I began to feel restless again. I managed to get to India and then to Cairo and then back to London again. On the night I arrived I went to the Savoy and there met most of the newspaper and radio people I knew. There was, they said, something in the air. They had had hints and heard rumours of the opening of a definite second front. Where or when they did not know, although there were countless guesses and a good deal of heated argument. But no one really knew anything.

And then one afternoon Thompson, who ran our London office, sent for me. In his office he said, " Dave, you're going to have the chance of a lifetime. Something big is up. I don't know exactly what but thousands of troops with all the equipment for an A Number One invasion are leaving to-night. I've fixed it for you to go with them."

" Where are they going ? "

" Don't ask me that . . . Holland, Spain, Norway, Dakar, Casablanca. . . . It might be anywhere. But you'll have to get out of here by the noon train from Waterloo if you're going. So scram ! You can stop back here for papers and things. They'll be ready for you."

I made it—the train, I mean—with not much time to spare. It was a correspondent's dream suddenly realized.

The rest is already history. I myself came ashore at Algiers and went to the Hotel Metropole. On the fourth day, at about noon, I went to the hotel desk on my way to the rather meagre lunch which was the best a country long pilfered by the Germans could offer. There was a message for me, and as I stood reading it a woman brushed past me and spoke to the man at the desk.

I think it was the voice that struck through my consciousness, a rather deep, warm voice, which I knew from somewhere, which I had not heard for years. Slowly it won my attention away from the message from Military Headquarters. I heard her asking whether it was yet possible to send out cables to America.

Then I turned and saw what appeared to be Annie Scanlon —Anna Bolton, yet a woman who was not Anna Bolton. She was thinner than when I had last seen her, yet the effect was not that of thinness but rather of warmth, almost of voluptuousness. She was dressed in cheap, provincial clothes, obvious copies of styles that had perhaps been fashionable in Paris three or four years earlier. Yet there was a *chic* about her that dominated the cheap material and the *démodé* quality of the cut of her clothes. She held the hand of a little boy three or four years old—an attractive, sturdy little fellow with dark hair and rosy cheeks and blue eyes.

My first impulse was to speak to her and then I thought, " I must be crazy or imagining things. It couldn't possibly be Annie Scanlon."

But the certainty was so great that I could not walk away. I think, too, there was something about the child that had its part in the vividness of the impression. The child looked like Tom Harrigan. He had the same radiance and health, that same manner of perfect adjustment to life even at the age of three. You would have noticed him anywhere.

Then an idea came to me. Aloud, as if to myself, I said, " Annie Scanlon ! "

The effect was immediate. She turned towards me and I knew at once the woman was Anna Bolton, yet as I saw her in full face there was something about her that was not Annie Scanlon, at least not the Annie I had known. The hard look was no longer in the eyes. There was no hardness about the mouth.

The experience was an extraordinary one.

She looked at me directly for a moment and then said, " Why, it's Dave. What are you doing here ? "

The voice was warm and filled with excitement, and I remembered suddenly the other cold Anna standing at the head of the great stairway in Haddonfield House.

I explained and said, " But it is more extraordinary to find you here. How did you get here ? "

She laughed. " That's a long story. I've been here for a long time. Why don't you come out for tea this afternoon ? You will, won't you ? " There was an eagerness in her voice.

" I think I can get there after five."

She took a bit of paper from a bloc that stood on the desk beside us and wrote something on it and handed it to me. I read :

Madame JEAN PIERRE LAMBERT,
Villa Mimosa
142 Rue des Acacias
Algiers 31ème

Then she said, " This is my stepson, Jean. *Dis bonjour, Jean.*"
The boy held out his hand and said, " *Bonjour Monsieur,*" politely.

" I'll see you then at five," I said.

" We'll have a lot to talk about. You've become very famous."

" You didn't do so badly yourself. For a long time in

London, what became of Anna Bolton was one of the principal topics of conversation."

She smiled and said, " That's all over. Don't tell anyone you saw me."

" It's not likely I'll see anyone here who knew you, but I won't say anything."

" Until this afternoon then."

A barouche drawn by a strange team, one a donkey and the other an ancient, thin, flea-bitten horse, took me to the Rue des Acacias. The street was as banal as its name, so far from the centre of the town that it might have been a suburb. It was a street lined with small, dull, unpretentious villas built during some prosperous period of the French administration, each with a wall shutting in a garden where acacias and mimosa grew. They were houses which were cheap but respectable, the kind that might be occupied by government clerks. The roadway, like everything else in Algiers, was dirty and in a bad state of repair after almost three years of German domination and Vichy administration.

The Villa Mimosa could not be distinguished from its neighbours save by the number and by a door in the garden wall on which the ancient paint had faded to a lovely dull turquoise colour. I promised the dirty Arab driver a fat fee to wait for me, since I saw no prospect of finding any vehicle in so remote a quarter and I had no desire to lose myself in Algiers under the chaotic conditions which existed in the city.

I got down and pulled the handle of the bell which jingled distantly in the garden. I thought, " This is a long way from Haddonfield House and the Ritz." And then the gate was opened by an Arab woman with a good deal of Negro blood. She was old but neatly dressed and clean. Inside, the garden was very well kept but there were few flowers and no grass—only rows of vegetables in various stages of growth. In a corner at the far end of the garden there was a row of rabbit hutches in which twenty or thirty rabbits were visible and near them a pair of she-goats with fat udders, one with a kid by her side, munched with a blank air of contentment at a bundle of weeds and tree branches.

Here, in a half-desert country that had been pilfered of

everything, the little scene inside the garden wall gave one a sense of plenty, almost of abundance.

"All that," I thought, "is Anna with her brain and energy. She could have run a factory or a bank."

Then the door opened and Anna herself stood there smiling at me.

"Well, this is it," she said, with a kind of pride, more pride of the proper kind than I had ever seen before in her.

"It's very cosy," I said, for that seemed exactly the word—a little universe on a small scale.

"It's all right," said Anna.

Inside, the house was neat and a little shabby, but what furniture there was had been arranged nicely. There was a little hall and off it a small *salon*. The cool that descends quickly in North Africa as the sun goes down had set in, and a small fire was burning in the fireplace. The Arab woman came in bringing tea and goat's milk and an assortment of those dry, hard little cakes that taste like cardboard, and some thin slices of black bread.

"There isn't any whisky," Anna said. "I could offer you some acid red wine but you wouldn't want to drink it. It's lucky our troops have come in. There just isn't anything left in the whole country. If you don't look after yourself you starve to death. It's been that way for a long time."

"You've got tea," I observed.

"That has drifted in from Casablanca—black market."

But I wanted to hear her story and I said so.

She laughed, "I'll tell you, but it's not to go any further than youself. Where shall I begin?"

"When the Germans came to Paris. I think I know the earlier part."

She gave me a sudden quick glance of suspicion and then haltingly she began to tell the story you have already heard, beginning with the flight from the Ritz which ended at Villiers with the tragedy by the roadside.

I watched as much as I listened, wondering at the transformation in Anna, realizing that the Anna I had known long ago could never have talked thus, more and more freely as she warmed to the story. It wasn't only that there was a remarkable physical change in her, as if she had grown up and become another woman ; there was a new freedom of spirit—the kind of thing you find only in people who have reached that peak of understanding at which even they themselves take on an objective quality. They have a special warmth; they are able to speak of themselves dispassionately, as if they saw themselves at a great distance.

"In the beginning," she said, "I was about ready for the end—bored, selfish, mean, bitter, with no roots and no place to go. I was a first-class trollop."

As she talked I saw that all the sullenness, the stiff-necked pride, the resentment which had deformed all her life and spirit, as disease can deform a bright and healthy body, was no longer there. She had found something which, without knowing it perhaps, she had always wanted, something that made the dull commonplace house, the black bread, the dry, hard little cakes, the boredom, the danger, all of no consequence whatever. It made of the drab little villa a palace and of the cakes and tea nectar and ambrosia.

While I listened to the story of Miss Godwin and her death, the stories of the wretched people in the brickyard, of Von Kleist and Madame Ritz, but most of all of Jean Pierre Lambert, the sun disappeared behind the Algerian hills and darkness came down quickly.

As she talked I saw that she understood what was going through my mind. Once she stopped the narrative and said, "I understand why you are staring that way at me. Sometimes I feel like staring at myself." She looked away from me and said almost with sadness. "You see, I am happy. I never knew what that was before. There was Tom, but that was a little thing which touched only ourselves. It was in a way a selfish thing which we found in each other. Nothing outside touched us. We lived in a kind of dream. I know now that it could not have lasted. This is different. This is something that cannot be destroyed. You see, I am . . ." she searched for words, " now I am a part of humanity itself."

"I understand."

She knew it too—that she was the most fortunate of people, that in her understanding, in utterly losing herself, she had gained a great treasure which very few people ever attain.

She came to that part of the story when in the broken-down bakery truck she set out from Gerbevilliers with the baby, Jean Lambert and the thin man called Jacques, not knowing whither she was bound or what lay at the end of the journey, not caring because she was in love.

"We drove nearly all night," she said. "The truck kept breaking down but the man called Jacques understood it as one understands a mule or a horse. He would tinker with it and get it going again and we would go a few miles before it broke down again. We got to Lyons a little before daylight and went to a hotel. It was crowded and we spent the rest of the night in chairs in the hall, and that afternoon we took the train to Marseilles. The false papers were very good for they were examined again and again by the manager of the hotel, by a police inspector, by the men at the railway station and by more police on the train. No one questioned them. They described *Monsieur et Madame Henri St. Genis et leur fils Jean Pierre*. Jean himself kept saying, "*Vive le Maréchal*," at proper intervals. By the time we reached Marseilles a curious thing had happened. We were married without ever having been married. It was as if we had been married for a long time and were perfectly happy. We understood each other. It wasn't even any longer necessary to pretend anything for the sake of the false papers.

"At Marseilles we had to wait two days for a transport ship bound for Oran. As a married couple the manager of the hotel gave us a single room and we went to it and spent those two nights and afterwards the two nights on the boat as Monsieur and Madame St. Genis, always as if we had always been married. The actual ceremony was carried out a week later in the little church of St. Vincent in Oran."

She laughed suddenly, "It was an odd courtship. There wasn't any proposal. There wasn't even any very formal declaration of love. It was as if it was meant to be, as if it had always been, as if we had no choice in the matter. It was, in a strange way, as if Tom had never died, as if he had only been away for a long time and come back to me. It makes me believe in strange things." She looked into the fire. "You see, now? You must know how right it is."

She was trembling and on the verge of tears. Then she looked at me suddenly. "Lewisburg is dead. The Flats are dead." She said suddenly, "You understand what I mean, Dave?"

"Yes, I understand. They're dead with me too. They have been for a long time."

" But it was worse with me—so much worse."

I knew what she meant. Then there was a little silence. By
now there was no light in the room save what came from the
fire. She stirred herself and lighted the wick of a Moorish lamp
that hung from the ceiling. The lamp gave out a feeble light
and the flame spluttered. In the semi-darkness I was seeing many
things, the Flats and the High School in Lewisburg, Haddonfield
House in London, now bombed and burned, the five-thousand-
franc *chemin-de-fer* room in Monte Carlo, empty now or fre-
quented by a few half-starved ghosts, poor old Miss Godwin
standing beside me as we looked down on the fireworks and
naked women on the barge at Monte Carlo, saying, " It won't be
long now." Certainly it was an incredible age in which we lived.

Then I said, " There's one thing I've wanted to ask you for
a long time."

" What ? "

" That night at Haddonfield House in London. Did you
know me or not ? "

In the dim light I could not make certain, but I had a feeling
that violent colour had come into her face. She said, " Yes, I
knew you, but you might have got in the way of things I
wanted then."

Silence hung in the room for a second. I had nothing to say,
but presently Anna, with a curious passion in her voice, said,
" But Anna Bolton is dead ! Annie Scanlon and Annie Harrigan
are dead ! There is only Anna Lambert ! So don't tell anyone
about me. I want to be left alone as Anna Lambert. Nobody in
the world knows what has become of Anna Bolton except yourself and my lawyer in New York. Anna Bolton disappeared in
France. Nobody knows whether she was killed or died in a
concentration camp. I want it to be like that. All the other
Annas are dead."

While she was speaking the bell in the garden jangled.
Apparently in her emotional state she hadn't heard it. It jangled
again now.

" There he is," she said, and rose to go over and open the door.

A big man in the uniform of the Engineers came into the room.
He kissed Anna and she said in French, " I have met an old friend
here from America. We went to school together." And
suddenly I was aware of a deep gratitude for having known
Anna and all her story.

[159]

He turned towards me and for a moment I had, in the dimly lighted room, the chilly sensation of being face to face with a ghost, or with something even more incredible than a ghost, for it seemed to me that Tom Harrigan was looking at me, Tom as he would have been perhaps if he had gone on living. But I knew, too, that this was something better than Tom would perhaps have been, for Tom, with all his charm and good looks and vitality, was a shallow fellow, in a groove. He could never have been like this one.

I heard Anna saying, " You see ? " And then softly in English in that warm new voice of hers, she said, " I am very grateful. God gave me another chance."